THE LEGACY

Mark Snyder Jr

CONTENTS

Title Page

Copyright

Introduction   1

Chapter 1 – The Legacy Members   3

Chapter 2 – The Donovans   27

Chapter 3 – Johanna's Grief   39

Chapter 4 – Revelation and Sacrifice   62

Chapter 5 – Movement   74

Chapter 6 – Arrival   85

Chapter 7 – Together   94

Chapter 8 – Burgeoning Friendship   111

Chapter 9 – Discovery   128

Chapter 10 – Ellen's Healing   137

Chapter 11 – Past Ties Revealed   146

Chapter 12 – Fawad's Revelation   162

Chapter 13 – Clayton's Position   168

Chapter 14 – The Donovans' Preparation   183

Chapter 15 – The Donovans' Guests   190

Chapter 16 – Azra's Opportunity   203

Chapter 17 – Fawad's Choices   214

Chapter 18 – Part of the Congregation   223

Chapter 19 – Azra's Acclimation   230

Chapter 20 – The Letter   240

Chapter 21 – Azra's Choices   251

Chapter 22 – New Beginnings   260

INTRODUCTION

G reek legend dictates that Aether, primordial god of the universe, separated its vastness into galaxies to maintain order and balance.

Hera, the powerful goddess of our galaxy, the Milky Way, and queen of all gods, organized her expansive domain into solar systems and each system was granted a great burning star, to rule and provide life.

Helios, the powerful god of the Sun and ruler of our solar system, designed each unique planet and presides over them. Helios was charged with the origination of life, in which he molded Gaia, the goddess of Earth, to keep life safe and provide it with a suitable and thriving home, the only life granting planet in our solar system.

Gaia's diverse ecosystems of life were eventually borne from the careful and methodical evolution of all living things. She granted humans the great intellect of mind, the intricate and complex composition of physical bodies, and the knowledge to prioritize the life of the planet, and of one another. These gifts of life were meant to aid humans in the protection of Gaia and of themselves.

Helios is protective over each of his planets, but

must ensure that his life-giving planet, Earth (Gaia), survives and maintains Aether's plan of a universe of balance. Helios is concerned for Gaia and will do anything to protect her. So begins the Legacy.

CHAPTER 1 – THE LEGACY MEMBERS

"But, it's too soon!" Finn said to himself in a hush so that Katherine wouldn't hear him.

"It's only August 8th!" Katherine heard his remark and Finn locked eyes with his wife as she tried to keep him from seeing her fear. His loving, large brown eyes always looked at his wife with the greatest sense of adoration and Katherine could always use Finn's eyes as an indicator of his emotions.

She had a lot on her mind as she began the labor process a few short hours ago, prior to their impromptu ambulance ride to the hospital. Katherine shrieked in agony, realizing she wasn't experiencing the normal labor pains of a woman about to give birth with no complications.

They had been shopping for a baby's crib when, all of a sudden, Katherine lost her balance and fainted. "You were quite conscious before you fell," she was informed by Finn as they carefully drove their way home from the store, but she had no recollection of the day's events up to beginning labor on the cold, hard tile of their bathroom floor. Katherine was only a few days into her seventh month of pregnancy, and with this being her first child and only just barely noticeably showing, they were already on edge about the arrival of the baby. Katherine was very slight in her physique, so most people who met her didn't notice that she was expecting.

Everything in their life was *always* thoroughly planned, as was their first date, engagement to be married, wedding, and renting their first, very modest apartment.

"How could this have happened? Do you remember having a *successful* night?" Katherine asked Finn while facing him, holding the home pregnancy test.

Finn responded with a great deal of embarrassment, "Of course, I...I think it was that time after dinner near the pier...I had wine that night, remember?" Finn was a tall, attractive young man who always saw himself as virile and capable. His inability to perform now that he was married was a complete mystery. He loved Katherine and wanted to share everything with her; it was as if his body was rejecting their sexual intimacy.

Katherine didn't remember that night being successful, at all. In fact, she remembered it being quite *unsuccessful*. That didn't matter to her, though, because she was deeply in love with her husband and they were both *very* inexperienced.

"The baby wasn't planned, so what? No one needs to know that small detail of our lives," she recalled Finn flippantly commenting. She tossed her used pregnancy test into the waste can and tried desperately not to fall to pieces in front of the young husband she so adored.

Katherine stared up at strangers while feeling the most intense pain of her life, in the back of an ambulance ping-ponging down a busy street during the height of the summer tourist season in Brighton. Katherine and her unborn baby's lives were in jeopardy, and the young couple's fears about the unplanned pregnancy just became their stark reality.

Li Jie

Li Jie sat on the side of his bed and thought about living the last one-hundred years, from 1935, beginning with the entirety of WWII and every conflict and major global event to follow, to the current year, the age of extreme modernity, convenience, and massive losses to the natural world. He prepared himself for bed and unfolded the starch-crisp, white bedsheets from their fixed and tucked ensemble. His face was still quite youthful in appearance, with the lines of a life well-lived, despite most of it being marred with sadness and tragedy. With the bustling activity of the busy Beijing streets below his apartment, Li Jie finished the letter he had begun writing many years ago, placed it within its simple, clean envelope, and closed his eyes for the very last time.

Eleven years ago, on his eighty-ninth birthday, Li

Jie received a letter and his life changed forever. He suffered from a heroin addiction that ruined his relationship with his son and depleted much of the retirement savings he worked so hard to collect throughout his working years. The night he was approached with the letter, Li Jie was going through a difficult withdrawal to try and end the destructive cycle of his potentially deadly habit.

There was a heavy knock at the door. "Who on Earth could that be?" Li Jie asked himself as the sweat rolled down his face, soaking the sheets under him in his bed.

The knocking, as it went unanswered, turned into banging, then what sounded like kicking, and finally, the door was forced open by a tall, young man. The man stepped out of the way to reveal a less intimidating but much older woman, who paid the man and slowly moved into Li Jie's small, dark and stuffy studio apartment.

The woman handed him a letter and instructed him to read it and take every word of it very seriously. She touched his clammy, pale face and apologized for her delay in delivering the letter, gently kissed his forehead, and exited the apartment through the door now hanging wide open.

As she passed through the damaged door frame, she stopped, turned around to face him, and said, "Li Jie, you must believe in, and act on, the instructions in the letter, for the sake of us all." The old woman slowly turned back to the hallway and continued to walk away.

Li Jie would have chased after the woman but he was weak and quite sick and had absolutely no strength to stand, let alone walk or run after her, though she was many years older than even he.

Li Jie's hands shook as he opened the folded letter to read its contents, each word seemingly written specifically to him from someone he'd never met. The letter discussed how his mother died in childbirth (during Li Jie's delivery), and that his father suffered a deep depression for most of his young life and eventually committed suicide when Li Jie was only fourteen years old, forcing him to raise himself from that point to today, his final day on Earth. Li Jie, beaten and scarred, as the letter discussed, was his birthright and the intended outcome of his entire existence was the ability to see the beauty in humanity, an outcome that was eventually realized.

Ellen

At the exact moment that Li Jie's eyelids closed, Katherine pushed so hard that she felt her organs shift, her bones crack and her breath grow shallow. Katherine knew exactly what had happened and what was about to happen; she understood that her newborn daughter had done irreparable damage to her delicate frame. Katherine looked down at her baby being cleaned, looked at Finn's doting eyes changing before her very own as he noticeably became aware of her fatal condition. Katherine was gone before she was able to hold her daughter and before she would ever learn her baby's name. Finn called for his wife as the light dimmed from her eyes while he held their newborn, premature, baby girl, and the air was completely sucked from the room. Finn named her Ellen, Katherine's middle name.

Clayton

Clayton woke in a panic. He was having the most vivid dream of shadowy figures laughing and celebrating. In the dream, Clayton would try to interact with the figures, but they would not materialize, as though he was seeing a group of blurred ghosts. The figures all rushed into a huddle, frantically shouting as the celebration shifted from jovial to alarming. Clayton was confused and lost as the figures in the dream crossed and scattered. The trauma of the dream must have caused a great deal of teeth clenching as Clayton's squarely shaped jaw was throbbing in a heavy, dull pain.

Today was an important day for the ambitious, bright-eyed nineteen-year-old, as he was beginning a new chapter of his life. A conversation with his mother several weeks ago helped Clayton decide it was time to act on his future rather than continue to look to a past barely remembered.

"I know this may be hard to talk about, but what would you say if I decided to go to culinary school, maybe be a chef, like dad was?" Clayton carefully asked his mother.

This question, from the son that she adored, stopped her in her tracks as she was setting the table for dinner. "I think that would have made your father very proud, Clayton," she responded and started to cry, sat down at the dining room table, and stared at the wedding ring on her left hand.

"You know, he was the best, and everyone knew it." She looked at Clayton while she spoke with tears running down her high cheek bones.

Clayton's father was a successful chef that served the privileged in Sydney, often cooking in exotic locations that included elaborate yachts and sprawling estates. His family lived on the southeastern coast of Australia, near the breathtaking views of the harbor where the rich and famous would entertain, host clients as well as throw lavish parties.

"I wish I could remember more about him, mah," Clayton said, acknowledging her sorrow.

"You were so young, Clayton, make your own memories of him, they're just as real," she replied, trying to make him feel better about being so young when his father left the house for the last time.

Clayton didn't know too much about his father, Jim, other than he was tall and thin, like Clayton. Jim mysteriously disappeared when Clayton was very young. He would often stop by the large photo of Jim that hung above the mantle in the living room and look into his father's big, trusting, brown eyes. This was the only father figure he really ever had, a portrait of a man he didn't remember ever meeting in person.

Clayton's mother would, every so often, retell the story of her husband's strange disappearance. The story seemed to help her get through times when she needed him most, especially these times of change as Clayton grew up and could have used his father's advice.

She always started the story the same way, "A few days after your fourth birthday, your father left to spend several days at sea on the yacht of a young heiress, the daughter of a world-famous jeweler, Frederik Faberge."

She hated the young woman that employed him during his final job, the job that took him from her, and she never described her in a positive light. Her name was Sonia Faberge. It would continue, depending on the severity of his mother's grief at the time, varying in length, detail, and tone, but the general story was always the same.

First, the biting remembrance of Sonia, "Sonia Faberge was a woman who dripped of self-assigned entitlement and a selfishness that was so engrained in her personality that she seldom realized when she was being unreasonable. Sonia was beautiful, but the kind of beautiful that only wealthy people were able to be, the kind of beauty that money could bring someone that was otherwise simply attractive." Clayton loved watching his mother tell this story and he could see how therapeutic it was for her to relive the events.

The night the yacht left its slip, Jim called his wife to tell her that the trip was underway, and he was preparing the menu for the next day. As expected, he expressed his frustrations with the never-ending list of demands from his most particular employer, a woman he often described as rivaling Narcissus, the Greek god of narcissism.

"Nothing seemed unusual about that day..." Clayton's mom, Sandy, would say, "...except for a feeling of slowly developing worry that I just shrugged off." Her words were shaky by this point in the story. "If only I had known, Clayton, if only I had paid closer attention."

Before Jim disappeared, Sandy was always worried when Jim left on the Faberge yacht, due to the terrible way he was treated and expected to serve Sonia and her friends without any room for his own thoughts and feelings... or dignity. To be completely honest, Sandy was also quite jealous of Sonia, as Jim was able to experience the polished, finer things in life while in her presence, even if he was just serving them and not actually *experiencing* them.

The rather large, and rather new, Faberge yacht disappeared on the second day of its voyage. Sonia had been very well-known in Australia, and her disappearance was immediately newsworthy. The search for the yacht was extensive but the boat was never recovered, despite it being one of the largest and most famous yachts in Australia.

Sonia moved through a group of people that were all very similar to one another; they took advantage of their place in society and had little regard for anyone who didn't know their way around a super-yacht. Needless to say, this particular voyage was meant to celebrate Sonia's engagement to another of Sydney's elite, a young real estate mogul with a face only a mother could love. He was given a financial boost by his uber-wealthy father and Sonia couldn't help but fall head over heels in love with *that* kind of money. No two people were better suited as they rivaled one another in superficiality and arrogance.

The yacht hosted eighteen well-dressed, well-connected, and valuable up-and-comers, and its unexpected disappearance rippled through the news cycle for many months. Clayton's mother mourned while no mention of her husband's name was ever uttered, until, that is, it was all anyone could talk about.

After the rumors began of a cook caught stealing from Sonia Faberge a year prior (an accidental oversight of paying double for a monthly food order), did the headlines begin to insinuate foul play, with Jim as the main player.

It was August 8th which marked a day that Clayton dreaded, as it was the anniversary of his father's disappearance. Each year, this anniversary would thrust Clayton back to his childhood, and he would relive those confusing feelings of chaos to a four-year-old, the only thing he could remember from that time in his life.

Today was also the first day of his choice to honor his father and follow in his footsteps of being a chef. Clayton was required to buy a chef's coat for his technical skills classes and had been studying how he looked in it, in the mirror, feeling proud of his decision but also hesitant of its emotional toll. The fifteenth anniversary of Jim's passing was not only difficult for him, but also for his mother.

Today was bittersweet for Clayton and his mother, "It's the bitter that comes before the sweet," Clayton's mother always told him when things weren't going his way. "Your father used to say that whenever I needed to hear it," his mother would remark each time.

The grief that came with the loss of his father seemed to only strengthen year after year. It was odd, but Clayton never accepted his father's death as a reality, almost as though he expected him to walk through the door, even after all these years.

Today, it was Sandy that needed the pep talk, so Clayton decided to check in on her before heading off to class. Clayton had a gentle way with his mother, she relied on him as much as he relied on her. Clayton provided a comforting solace that she couldn't describe in words, but she always felt the persistent connection between mother and son, especially this connection that was forged out of tragedy. There was another young man, many miles away, for whom Clayton would share an unknown kinship of early grief.

Ameer

Ameer was also nineteen years old, but, unlike Clayton, lived with his father. Ameer was seven when his mother was taken from the modest family home, and he remembered that day through the filter of his emotions. There was panic, anxiety, fear, anger and confusion all swirling through the house and this rush of emotions was felt by himself as well as his father.

Ameer remembered the day his mother was taken, and he held onto his memories, trying desperately to never forget. His father was taken to be questioned at the police station. It was most common for women to be sold by someone close to them, such as a spouse or an older male child. When his father returned from his interrogation, after being gone for the entire day, he was in no mood to comfort the little boy, desperately trying to figure out what happened to his mother.

His father seemed to be keeping something from Ameer, but to this day, he never asked for the complete story of his mother's disappearance. Ameer knew she had never told him that she was leaving, and always wondered why a mother would simply abandon her son. He knew that his father was both violently angry and woefully grieving at the same time and Ameer spent most of that day hiding from his father. In the end, the story that was given to Ameer from his father and his extended family, was that his mother was kidnapped and assumed dead.

Ameer was very much like his father, stubborn and assertive. Every time he would attempt to ask further questions, his father would change the subject in a choked up and erratic episode of impatience and extreme defensiveness. Ameer assumed that it was just too difficult for his father to revisit that day, and he shared that pain. There was a hole in Ameer's gentle heart, and he wished he had the answers to bring him peace about her mysterious disappearance.

Ameer hated that he was like his father in so many ways. As the two men grew further and further apart, Ameer became a fierce and brave advocate for human rights due to his mother's believed abduction from the family home, which enraged his conservative father. Ameer shared the strong brow that masked as confidence, on both men, and as Ameer's father grew older, the look wavered with his burdened, sad eyes.

Clayton and Ameer were thousands of miles apart but shared an important relationship that only two people on the planet would ever share, together, at the same time. Most importantly, though, was that only one of these young men would ever discover their connection existed at all.

Sarah

"What's the plan for tonight?"

Sarah's mother attempted to catch the attention of her daughter before she spent another day upstairs hiding from her parents.

It was August 8th, in a suburban neighborhood of Baltimore, Maryland, where the lawns are groomed, the bushes are trimmed, the Smiths know the Millers, and they both know everyone else. Sarah had only a few days left of summer break before she would go back to school and finally get out from under the oppressive and nagging thumb of her opinionated mother.

Tonight, was the annual end-of-summer family gathering and it was entirely expected that she be in attendance. Sarah was only eleven years old, but her eyes looked as though she had lived many lifetimes, and she carried this weight on her shoulders each day, completely alone. Sarah was tall, very pale and never felt connected to other children her age, due to her melancholy as well as her looks.

She couldn't remember ever being young and carefree like her classmates. She would sometimes wake up and greet the day with promise and gratitude, then, just as suddenly, sense a mind-numbing sorrow. These extreme shifts in mood had been diagnosed by many doctors as *acute bipolar disorder.*

"Of course, it is very uncommon to have such a severe case in a child," muttered the last insensitive doctor her mother dragged her to, to get what seemed like the one-hundredth opinion.

Sarah didn't care what it was labeled, and she didn't have an explanation for anyone who asked, as her mother so often did. She did know she was wildly happy at times and tragically mournful at others. She would be frozen with worry one moment, and then immediately loose with the feeling of the greatest security, the next. This was her life at the young age of eleven, so she decided to be alone to shield herself as much as possible from any outside influences that could trigger her. Sarah felt as though she was destined to live a life of extremes that would develop at the drop of a hat and disappear just as fast as they began. The only small indicator for the quality of her days was her dreams.

Many nights, Sarah would silently sit in her room and spend hours documenting her dreams and her mood swings in a private journal. She would try to detect the patterns of her behavior in an attempt to prepare for the periods of self-imposed isolation.

Sarah's dreams, when she could remember them, weren't like her mood swings at all. In fact, on nights when her dreams were relatively mild and uneventful, her days were wracked with the manic highs and depressing lows that plagued her life.

Sarah would dream about many things, but there were some recurring situations. There was a woman that Sarah often watched in her dreams who was always running away from something. Sarah would be above her, looking down, watching this woman cry alone in a dark room illuminated only by the thinnest sliver of moonlight. She would sometimes see the woman running in fear, constantly looking behind herself as she flailed and stumbled while she ran. This woman was sometimes joined by a boy who looked similar to her. He would reach for her, but she would only turn and run from him as well, looking fearful.

There were others that Sarah would see in her dreams; a young man would also see Sarah as she observed him. He would just look and smile at her, sometimes mouthing words as though he was talking to her, but she was never able to hear him. Sometimes the young man was joined by a little girl who was very sad but had the most radiant green eyes though they were often bloodshot from crying.

Sarah began to detect the patterns to her conscious behavior; when she remembered these dreams or visits during her sleeping hours, she knew her day would be manageable. She knew she could bury her thoughts long enough to talk to her mother and smile through most of her interactions with adults at school and at home. Eventually, Sarah began to feel as though the people that she could see in her dreams were real, and she looked forward to them coming to her. She felt as though she needed them, and perhaps they needed her.

Sarah's mother didn't understand her daughter's issues, no one could, not even Sarah. Sarah's mother was very focused on her appearance and frustrated with Sarah's stringy hair and sallow complexion. It would seem logical to look up her behavior in the Diagnostic and Statistical Manual of Mental Disorders (DSM) and compare the signs of Sarah's behavior to a clinically defined illness, but that had proven to be an exercise in futility.

The counseling, the medications, the frustrations, had all proven ineffective. Sarah was unaware that thousands of miles away in South Africa lived another who would understand her struggles. Someone who had lived far longer with these issues and had let them permanently change her.

Johanna

The sun was slowly making its way across the horizon as it inched closer and closer to presenting another day to the planet. Johanna feared the new day, and each day this fear grew more and more unbearable.

Johanna would often use this time before sunrise to take a long look at herself in the mirror. Her face showed the weather of her life on it, even through the warmth of her smooth, caramel colored skin. Her eyes were surrounded by dark circles created by the stains of years of sleeplessness and exaggerated by the long and heavy, unmanaged black hair on her head.

Johanna had been living a mostly nocturnal life since she reached her mid-thirties, when she realized just how difficult it was to be awake with the majority of society. She noticed that her emotions were far more unpredictable during the day so each morning at sunrise, she would take her daily dose of Xanax with a bourbon chaser. Melatonin used to be enough to settle her mind. Soon after, it was over-the-counter sleeping pills, which then led to a prescription from her doctor, and now, even that was almost totally ineffective on its own.

Her dangerous cocktail of opiates and alcohol was a relatively new strategy, but it was working. Johanna would find that watching dreadful morning television as her mind and body started shutting down from its forced poisoning, was calming to her. There were a few minutes before unconsciousness that she actually *felt* human; it was after the beginning warm buzz but before the almost comatose drooling stage of the daily sleep ritual. She clung to that feeling, as she knew it was the only time in her entire day that she would be at peace. As of now, this brief moment of hope was the only thing keeping her alive.

Twelve years ago, Johanna was found wandering around the streets of the Nyanga neighborhood of Cape

Town. She had no memory of her life prior to the weeks she spent recovering from severe dehydration, malnourishment and what was explained to her as repeated and violent sexual assault. As she laid in her hospital bed, Johanna recalled images of a small child and a place that looked different from her current surroundings, but those were really the only clues she had to remind herself of who she was prior to being in the hospital.

"What is your name, dear?" a pleasant voice with a kind, round face muttered to her once she regained consciousness.

"Uh-well, I...I just don't remember," she said in response with a startled look on her face. It was the first time she had spoken since she regained consciousness. Johanna felt as though she had her entire life on the tip of her tongue, but just couldn't say the words; her memories were locked behind a door of self-protection.

She was surprised when she heard her voice — it was different from the nurse's voice with whom she was speaking. She had a very pronounced accent, but it was new to her, and so were the words in her mind. She would sometimes think in a different language and also began using those words in her speech. The doctor (who was a second-year resident at the hospital) told her she was speaking in Urdu, a language found primarily in Pakistan and India. He also explained to her that she had the complexion and features of someone from that part of the world. This information was both helpful and frustratingly puzzling for Johanna, bringing even more questions of her former life to the forefront of her mind.

Johanna was admitted to a hospital where trafficked women were brought quite regularly. There were several staff members, Johanna's nurse as well as her primary doctor, who helped victims of trafficking receive new identities and safe places to live in South Africa through connections they had to government employees.

Johanna watched many women come and go through the hospital during her stay, from the mildly sick with a virus or infection, to extreme cases of abuse and murder. There were girls as young as nine years old crying out for their parents, and older, weathered women who had been living on the streets for longer than they could remember.

They arranged new identification numbers, applications and approvals for disability pay to help the women get on their feet once they were discharged from the hospital as well as pay for their medical care, which helped to keep the hospital functioning. The essential documents, such as passports and birth certificates, were also provided so they could begin again with a new identity, or simply get back to where they were living prior to their abduction, as long as it was safe to do so.

The hospital received more trafficked women looking for refuge and medical care than any other type of patients. It was located just outside the region where Johanna was found stumbling, barefoot, wondering where she was, where she had been and how long had she been there.

The hospital was inconspicuous, within a building that contained a storefront as well as several apartments. The store was converted into a large room that held many beds and the apartments were equipped for surgery and other procedures that may be needed. The neighborhood in which the hospital was located was littered with trash and was a hotbed for gang violence and drug trafficking. The houses that surrounded the hospital were barely dilapidated huts with far too many people living in each of them.

Through this neighborhood of oppression, though, was this hospital that operated on the fringes of society, that helped women erase trauma from their lives and removed all traces of abuse, which often included abortions for those who were pregnant by their attackers.

When Johanna arrived at the hospital, she was pregnant. The child had died in the womb, most likely from malnourishment. Johanna was very thin and weak; it was obvious that she hadn't had anything to eat or drink for a very long time. She had a broken left cheek bone and bruises covered her thin body.

The young doctor explained to her that victims of such severe trauma often suffered amnesia that eventually subsided, and her memory should eventually return. He also told her the facial injury she received may have contributed to the memory loss, that perhaps the blow was powerful enough to inflict brain damage.

Johanna developed a friendship with her kind nurse, who was always speaking to her with a gentle, warm tone that brought her comfort when she needed it most. Her nurse would sit with her, hold her hand, brush her hair and tell her stories of how she had seen many women come and go from the hospital and live long and productive lives. "I just know you are special, dear," she would tell Johanna, and Johanna would smile, desperately wanting to believe her.

Over the weeks of her refuge from the trauma which she had since forgotten, Johanna was still and calm in mind and body as she regained her physical strength. Her memory would never fully return while she rehabilitated, and the images of the young child disappeared almost entirely from her thoughts as she focused on setting herself up with a new life once she was strong enough to leave the hospital. On the day of her discharge from that bleak, yet fondly remembered hospital bed, she was given an identification number and a new passport with the name of her beloved nurse, Johanna.

Sarah

Sarah heard the commotion of the family reunion downstairs. She always felt so different from her parents but found small comforts in some of her extended family. Sarah was the natural child of her parents, but her extended family members were not blood related. Her parents described a life in which they were both raised in military families (all four of her grandparents now deceased) and developed their slight accents, that Sarah just couldn't quite place, during these extended stays in different parts of the world. Sometimes, she would hear her parents talking in a hushed, thicker dialect, but she never asked her parents to explain; it was something she'd been hearing her entire life and really didn't think to go to the trouble of asking.

"Sarah, your family is asking for *YOU!*" belted her mother from the bottom of the stairs. "They think you've gone missing or something," she continued, hoping for a response from her daughter.

"Don't make us look like criminals and kidnappers, young lady!" was added in an afterthought with a much sharper, demanding tone.

Sarah wasn't having a bad day and her thoughts were actually quite calm, so she made her way downstairs to greet the family that she, for the most part, was happy to see again.

Just as Sarah was making her way downstairs, she stopped a few steps from the bottom. She was hit with a sorrow so intense it almost made her physically ill, as if her body received a sudden injury and her mind an instant shock. She had a brief vision of woman crying, holding a pistol to her head. The woman was alone in the dark, with the exception of that familiar sliver of moonlight illuminating her face. The vision was short, but so intense that Sarah could actually see the lines on the woman's face and the cold, reflective steel of the gun. As soon as the vision came to her, though, it was gone. It was a brief vision, something she had never experienced before, but it was palpable, and it was *frightening*.

In a state of unfamiliar shock, Sarah made her way to the backyard patio where her family cheered her arrival (the family was just talking of making it a point to boost Sarah's self-esteem with her all too public issues). While she stared blankly at them, hearing only muffled sounds and then seeing them swirl and dance around her, she fell upon herself like a marionette puppet whose puppet master had cut her strings. The family stood silent, dumbfounded, before erupting in frenzied calls to 911 while bending to tend to the limp pile of Sarah's lifeless body. Sarah's parents stood there, motionless, glancing at their daughter, then at each other, and back again to where she lay. Sarah's mother covered her face with her hand before coming to her senses and pulling her husband to the side of their unconscious daughter.

CHAPTER 2 – THE DONOVANS

Ellen

Finn and Ellen were living an almost entirely isolated and silent life together, which was not an easy thing to do in the busy resort town of Brighton, on the south-eastern coast of England. This isolation stunted Ellen's early development as a verbal communicator. They lived in the same apartment that had been shared by Finn and Katherine before Ellen was born.

She really didn't speak too often and when she did speak, it was just a few words in a quiet and breathy voice. Ellen was six years old now and getting ready to attend public school, a year later than her peers. Occasionally, Finn would briefly realize that Ellen needed more than he was giving her as a father, and he would attempt to engage her in conversation he imagined a father should have with his daughter.

"Hey, Ellen, do you think we should get a dog?" Finn questioned Ellen, wondering if she would get excited about the prospect of having a pet in the house, and he thought maybe it would cheer him up as well.

"No, daddy...I don't think so," Ellen replied, without turning her head away from the television.

"Why not? Don't you want something to take care of around here?" he pushed her a little further with an attempt at a jovial lilt in his voice.

"I already have something that I take care of, daddy," she responded with no lilt in her voice, in fact, no inflection at all.

"Oh, well that's a bit harsh, wouldn't you say?" Finn tried to get some semblance of a laugh from his daughter.

Ellen didn't bother to respond to his last comment.

"Okay, never mind then," he conceded and went back to reading the book that he'd been struggling to read for months now. This was, all too often, the same result of each conversation he attempted to initiate with his daughter.

Ellen was beginning to look more and more like her mother, and it was distracting Finn from his ability to think of *anything* other than Katherine. Finn's daughter's wavy golden hair would catch him off-guard at times, thinking his young wife had returned from wherever she went on that fateful day, six years ago, after her petite frame was shattered by her baby during childbirth.

Finn would see his daughter emerge from her bedroom for the day, and there were times that he thought he saw Katherine for just a split-second. "Katherine...I... I mean, Ellen...what's for breakfast?" Finn would often begin addressing his daughter by his wife's name before correcting himself and apologizing to her.

This resemblance, as it grew and grew by the year, helped push Finn into a deep depression that transformed this once vibrant and creative man into a shell that had been hollowed by the loss of his innocent wife. He was barely able to do the minimum amount of work to simply keep his daughter alive, and he also forgot she was required to go to school. Finn was only an imitation of a man, whose skin and clothes hung off of his forgotten body and all memories were lost of what happiness once was.

After Katherine's death, Finn blamed himself. He felt that since he was the one who made her pregnant, that he was also the one who killed her. Since then, Ellen also began to develop a sense of responsibility for her mother's death. Finn would often lose his temper (by no fault of Ellen's) and callously relive the day Ellen was born, and Katherine had died, August 8th, not realizing Ellen would begin to associate her birthday as the day she killed her mother. Ellen no longer had a birthday, only a day she feared and regretted.

Finn was not strong enough to be a father and Ellen was too young to protect herself from suffering the effects of this neglect. As soon as Ellen was out of the house and in school for the majority of the day, Finn made a pledge to kill himself and leave behind the daughter that reminded him so much of his beloved wife.

Ellen just got home from school, excited to tell her father about her first day, with an almost promising overtone of joy to her voice, hoping that it would cheer him up.

"Daddy, are you home...dad?" Ellen said as soon as she entered the house, hoping that he was standing by the front door to ask her about her day. Finn had not responded to her calls.

There was no answer, instead she was greeted with the foul smell of death in the apartment. It wasn't a smell she recognized as one thing or another, but she knew it wasn't supposed to be in her home.

Ellen walked toward the kitchen, holding the papers Finn needed to read and sign before the end of her first week at school. She stopped and followed the trail of her father's blood, brain matter, bone, and skin scattered from the ceiling, to the wall, and then to the floor by his body.

Ellen dropped everything she was holding and hid in her bedroom until the school called the next day when she didn't arrive. She told the secretary her father was dead in the kitchen and she needed someone to come get her.

She would only get to be near her father one last

time, the day his coffin was slowly lowered into the ground at his funeral.

After Finn's death, Ellen was passed around countless foster homes, growing more and more introverted, stunted and, at times, violently angry. She still wasn't talking very much, but her behavior became irrational when she finally allowed her voice to be heard. The last three years shaped Ellen into someone who couldn't love, couldn't trust, and had no sense of security or self-worth.

Each temporary home gave up on her, time and time again, pushing her further into feelings of unworthiness, guilt and disgrace. She believed she murdered her mother on her birthday and she caused her father to commit suicide. Ellen was starting to believe she brought tragedy and bad luck wherever she went.

"I just can't live with a child that scares me," and "I am afraid that she will murder me in my sleep!" were comments Ellen would hear as she was being collected and reassessed for new living arrangements.

Ellen often relived her mother's delivery or her father's suicide as she had pictured these events in her mind. She spent so much time thinking about the deaths of her parents, that she built alternate realities through these constructed memories, which would set off violent, out-of-the-blue tantrums of regret and self-blame.

Her next family, the Donovans, were noticeably different, though. They weren't afraid of this child, in fact, they seemed to be anticipating the challenge. Ellen remembered the day she met the Donovans. Usually, the new foster parents would meet her in a neutral place, or a place of comfort for the child, but the Donovans insisted Ellen be brought to their home.

When she arrived, the Donovans met Ellen and her current social worker outside of their home in Brighton, just a short drive from the apartment that Ellen shared with her father.

Mr. and Mrs. Donovan were tall and attractive, very well-groomed, and only spoke to the social worker, never looking at Ellen or speaking directly to her.

"Ellen needs to know that she will have nothing but safety and security in our home." Mrs. Donovan spoke as though she was interviewing for a job, not taking in a child.

Mr. Donovan joined his wife, "Stability is paramount in our household, it's the foundation of any family."

Unfortunately, a roof and four sturdy walls would be the only stability Ellen would receive from the Donovans. The Donovans officially adopted Ellen soon after taking her into their home as a foster child, and they moved her from the jovial and progressive seaside town of Brighton, to a small, conservative, and repressed, town in the American state of Colorado.

Alamosa, Colorado was a rural community with a population of approximately nine-thousand people and was the perfect place to take Ellen, as the Donovans were going to try to recondition her into *their* child. The Colorado skies were always crystal blue and the mountain views were breathtaking, but Ellen rarely saw their beauty due to the way her world looked to her, inside the walls of the Donovan house. They wanted to erase Ellen's former impressions of the world and replace them with new ideas of devotion, religion, sacrifice and humility.

The Donovans bought a small, mostly inoperable farm where they planned to be completely self-sufficient and teach Ellen how a life of servitude and sacrifice would lead to the unlimited fruits of Heaven. This dogmatic way of living would certainly be a shift for Ellen as she had very little education on any sort of devout ideologies. She hadn't been to school very much during her lifetime, so far, but when she was able to go, she always attended the local public schools of her foster homes. Religion was only something brought up in passing, or as a part of a holiday, not as the guiding force for everyday life.

Ellen, so far, had kept to herself in the Donovan home and kept away from making any negative impressions with her new parents. They seemed quiet as well, but a different *kind* of quiet she didn't recognize, one that was a disguise for a person hiding their true self. Ellen was only nine years old and she had limited interaction with adults, due to her father's death and her constant rotations through foster homes, but she could tell she still didn't know these people. That was soon about to change.

Several uneventful weeks had passed since the Donovan family moved to have a stronger *influence* on the life of their newly adopted daughter as well as have her live more in-line with their religious faith.

It was early one morning at breakfast, the Donovans requested that Ellen only call them Mother and Father. Since their first meeting, she had been calling her new parents Roger and Mary. She was not allowed to use the warmer, more familiar terms like dad or mom, as these terms "are disrespectful to the seriousness of their positions within the conditioning of her relationship to God," remarked Mrs. Donovan during an unexpected discussion that would begin Ellen's indoctrination into her new parents' religious piety.

The Donovans were always dressed for company, although no one ever came to visit before the church was built. Mother didn't wear makeup, and kept her dark brown hair tightly pulled back with a perfectly straight part in the middle of her head; and Father was a handsome middle-aged man, still in very good physical shape. He too, fashioned a perfectly straight part, and never allowed the slightest stubble to litter his skin.

It was after dinner, soon after their one-month anniversary of arriving at the farm, they sat Ellen down and provided her with the new rules of the Donovan household.

Ellen followed the couple into the small, empty, echoey living room where the sounds of three pairs of footsteps mimicked a small tap-dance ensemble. Mr. Donovan's steps were slower and his strides longer, Mrs. Donovan walked hard, with an almost exaggerated sound as if she was meaning to create as much noise as possible, and Ellen's were smaller steps, faintly heard between the loud clacks. Ellen was directed to sit on the wood floor while the Donovans took a seat on the dusty sofa, the only furniture in the room. The room was completely dark with the exception of the light from the hallway; the only lightbulbs in the entire house were in the downstairs and upstairs hallways.

"Ellen, now that you have been fortunate enough to be welcomed into our family and our new home..." uttered Mrs. Donovan in a very soft voice. She then cleared her throat and looked at her husband who hadn't taken his eyes off of Ellen. "We should now talk about how we expect you to behave, the situation of your schooling, as well as your obligation to assist in the maintenance of the farm."

Ellen understood the words coming from Mrs. Donovan's mouth and nodded silently in agreement, but slowly felt the room getting colder and darker than when she was directed to sit on the floor.

"You are only to speak in this house when you are requested to speak," Mr. Donovan blurted out as though he just wanted to get it over with, yet in an angry and unkind tone.

"And you will ALWAYS do *everything* that we tell you, without question or hesitation," followed Mrs. Donovan.

"You will be homeschooled by Mrs. Donovan every day after you finish your morning chores, and you will receive dinner every evening but only after completing your evening chores."

The Donovans continued with a strange back and forth list of rules that were slowly making Ellen feel as though she had just seen a ghost.

The rules continued on for a few more minutes and ended with, "You will respect our religion and *never* discuss anything that happens in our home with anyone outside of our home."

Ellen shook her head in agreement again, but this time, she opened her small mouth to use her faint, soft voice to inquire, "I've never been on a farm before, what kinds of chores are you going to make me do?"

Just as Ellen finished her sentence, she knew at once that she had made a mistake. The Donovans looked as though they had been slapped across the face. "Not even one minute after we finish our explicit discussion on the rules, do you immediately break them!"

Mrs. Donovan added, "I think we are dealing with more than we had originally expected!"

"We knew you would be bad!"

"We were told how deceitful you were!"

"I tried to deny to myself that a child could actually drive her father to commit suicide!"

"Haven't you learned anything about redemption after killing your mother?"

"You need to learn, tonight, that we will teach you with a heavy and consistent hand!"

During these verbal lashings, Ellen began to silently cry. The only way the Donovans could tell that she was crying was because of the tears streaming down her face. Her facial expression had not changed, nor was she making a sound, as more and more tears fell from her chin and cheeks and onto the wooden floor. Just then, Ellen was forced to lay on her stomach with her nose, chin and forehead touching the hard, dirty boards. The wood smelled of a musty earth and it was obvious this house had stood vacant for quite some time.

"This is your bed tonight," Mr. Donovan growled through his teeth, forcing spit to fly from his lips.

Just then Ellen felt a hard kick to her ribs with the pointed toe of Mrs. Donovan's shoe. This made Ellen cry with a writhing pain that forced her body to contort and the sounds of her weeping to echo off the walls of the cold, dark room.

"That's better," said Mrs. Donovan as matter-of-factly as possible.

Then, the loud taps moved out of the room and left Ellen alone to mentally work through what just happened to her. She had never been physically abused, even with the worst of her foster parents. She had many regular admonishments due to her silence and anger, and their frustrations, but she wasn't able to understand what just occurred. Ellen previously learned fear, sadness and loss, but she hadn't yet learned to feel abused. That education started this night, on the floor, in her new home.

Eventually, Ellen fell asleep after she acclimated to the stabbing pain from the broken ribs she had just endured. She brought herself some comfort thinking of what it might have been like to have had a mother and father that she could call mommy and daddy. She closed her eyes and asked her father to look over her, and that made her feel better.

CHAPTER 3 – JOHANNA'S GRIEF

Li Qiang

Li Qiang, Li Jie's seventy-one-year-old son, was making his way home within the Wan Chai neighborhood of Hong Kong, where he relocated from Beijing, nine years after his father's death. This neighborhood was attractive to him as it was often considered the "heart of Hong Kong," rich in the arts and always very clean and safe. These years without his father hadn't been easy; his father became his most trusted companion and they grew quite close during the last years of his life.

He was still grieving for his father, remembering how kind and peaceful he became later in his life. Li Qiang had gotten carried away at dinner, drinking Tsingtao (a beer he often shared with his father) and pulled out the envelope he retrieved from the bedside table of his father, examining the small parcel with intrigue. He held onto this letter since his father's death, as he was instructed to do.

He began weeping, thinking of the day he arrived at his father's apartment in Beijing and discovered his body on the morning of his one-hundredth birthday. Li Jie was lying on his bed just as though he was asleep. Li Qiang was surprised at how peaceful and serene he looked, with a warm and soft expression on his face. He composed himself and saw the letter his father mentioned on his bedside table. He carefully tucked the letter into his pocket and visited with his father for a while before calling the police to report his death. Li Qiang snapped out of his somber thoughts when the owner of the restaurant asked if he'd like another beer. He declined and began to make his way out of the restaurant and into the humid night air.

As he made his way home, his head was swimming with memories of his father and the idea that someone would eventually find him, someone he wouldn't know, but would know him. The tension of not yet being able to carry out this father's dying wish was eating away at him, which caused him to drink and smoke more than any other time in his life. Li Qiang transformed from a healthy, attractive older man, to an overweight and jaundiced elderly man in only nine years.

While walking through an empty alley he often used to stagger home, he stopped after hearing footsteps behind him, to look toward the sound. Suddenly, he was knocked to the ground with a violent blunt force to his head. As he lay in the middle of the road, in the early hours of the morning, his attacker was rifling through his jacket and pockets while a warm stream of blood began to run into his eyes and mouth. Right before losing consciousness, Li Qiang felt his father's letter being taken from his inside jacket pocket.

As Li Jie approached his one-hundredth birthday, he asked his son an unusual request, "I will need you to do me a favor after I die."

"Oh...most certainly, anything, I...will do anything," said Li Qiang, thinking that this was an ominous and strange thing to say but also seeing the deep conviction in his father's eyes.

"You must be the first person to enter my apartment on my one-hundredth birthday." Li Jie continued, "I will need you to collect a letter from my bedside after I pass." As he spoke his son looked at him with a somber face.

"After you pass?" Li Qiang repeated with surprise. "What's going to happen on your one-hundredth birthday?" he questioned, dreading his father's answer.

"That is the day that I am destined to die, son, as described to me in a letter that I received several years ago," Li Jie admitted to his noticeably skeptical son. "Promise me you will keep the letter in a safe place, that you will not open the letter, and you will be ready to give the letter to the right person when they request it." Li Jie spoke with more authority than his son had ever heard before.

"How will the right person know that I have your letter?" Li Qiang continued, "Why hasn't this person already collected your letter?"

"This person will be drawn to you *because* you have the letter, and in order for my purpose to be realized, I must only provide them with the letter *after* my death," Li Jie said with a great passion in his voice, enough to convince Li Qiang to listen to his father without interrupting.

As Li Qiang lay bleeding and drifting in and out of consciousness, he recalled this fateful conversation he had with his father when he was confided in as the only person he could trust to ensure that this seemingly important letter would make it to its intended recipient. Now, it was taken from Li Qiang by a violent stranger, a stranger that may simply discard it without a second thought, not realizing it was not only a letter, but the last promise he made to his father.

Johanna

Johanna woke just as the sun was setting, jolted out of bed due to a nightmare she was having that left her filled with an emptiness so intense that it took her a moment to catch her breath. The small child reappeared in her dreams for the first time since her admittance to the hospital. The little boy was crying and looking around for something, or someone. For the first time, she noticed he had the same dark hair and smooth complexion as she had. She tried to reach him, but he just kept moving further and further away. There were other people in this dream, not just the child, strange men that she didn't recognize. The men in the dream were laughing while she was crying out for the child as he disappeared from her view.

Johanna lived her life in seclusion and fear, only thirty or so kilometers from the hospital that saved her life. She was so very tired of the daily pain, the mood swings of pure elation to the devastating terror that paralyzed her and prevented her from living a normal life. Johanna decided to try and end the pain, again, and took a handful of Xanax with half a bottle of nighttime cough medicine, then picked up her cold steel gun from under the mattress in her dark, mostly empty, apartment.

Her gun was her only acquaintance. Every night for many years now, Johanna would contemplate using her gun as her forgotten past haunted her and her present was forcing her to be a recluse, hidden from the world. She would sit, idly, by the window when the moon was bright and high in the night sky, shaking, crying and wishing she could remember.

She took the gun to the roof of her apartment building and laid on her back staring up at the stars. The sky was brighter than usual that night. Each star was speaking directly to Johanna and her head became as full of the voices of the stars as though she was at a noisy party full of shouting people. Some stars were telling her to kill herself, some were complimenting her on her bravery and others were telling her to leave this place and go find him.

"Who is *him*?" she began to shout.

"WHO IS HIM!?" she screamed as loud as she possibly could, causing far off dogs to bark and lights to turn on in apartments nearby.

Johanna got onto her knees, picked up her gun and began weeping, sobbing so hard that she couldn't catch her breath. She placed the small, cold barrel of the gun to her head.

"Who isss... himmm..." she slurred as the cocktail of chemicals began to take effect and the stars began to swirl and bounce.

Just then, Johanna passed out, face first on the roof of the building, dropping her gun and plummeting into one of the deepest sleeps she had ever slept.

The boy came again to Johanna in her sleep, but his face was difficult to see. He was trying to speak to her, reaching for her again while she was being held back by the men surrounding her. The boy was mouthing words at first, but then she began to faintly hear his words.

"Hon..g ...ong" she could barely hear what he was saying.

"Hong ...ong" his words became more and more intelligible.

"Hong Kong," she finally heard what he had been

trying to say.

"What about Hong Kong? What do you mean Hong Kong?" she screamed in desperation to the little boy.

"Hong Kong!" he again said to her, but this time screaming at the top of his little lungs with the scream you would expect from a little boy trying to awaken his parents when he thought he saw the boogey man under his bed.

"I don't understand!" she screamed, waking herself up in the hot sun on the roof of her apartment building. Her mouth was completely barren of moisture and she had a piercing headache that made it impossible for her to see clearly.

Once Johanna fully regained consciousness, she collected her gun and made her way back to her apartment.

"I have to go to Hong Kong, I...just have to go," Johanna said to herself as she walked down the stairs to her apartment from the roof access door.

This wouldn't be the first time Johanna heard voices that told her to travel somewhere. She had a long history of what her doctor told her were schizophrenic episodes brought on by drugs and alcohol coupled with a severe lack of sleep. Johanna always listened to the voices that spoke to her, even though they lied to her. They were, really, all that she had in this world.

Immediately, she packed some belongings and her passport and raced to the airport to catch the next flight to Hong Kong. It took almost all the money she had to purchase the plane ticket, as she only received a small allowance of disability pay from the government, but nothing would stop her from reaching the boy in her dream. Perhaps this boy would be able to provide answers about her past life, she thought as she fidgeted in the security line. She didn't know what she was going to do when she arrived, but that wasn't important to her. This draw to Hong Kong was so powerful that she almost felt as though someone else was controlling her body; there was no hesitation and no second guessing.

As soon as Johanna arrived in Hong Kong, she walked through the airport and began frantically looking for the boy.

"I'm here, I'm here!" she shouted near the ground transportation waiting area.

"Where are you?" she began to cry and repeated it until she was approached by airport security.

"Ma'am, you...ok, you need...help?" the guard asked Johanna in broken English, he was noticeably shaken by Johanna's behavior.

"No, I came here to find the boy in my dream, he's here waiting for me, he's waiting for me!" she frantically responded to the guard's question.

The guard could tell Johanna was not completely stable at the moment and thought she may be a danger to herself, or others, if she wandered out of the airport shouting for some mysterious boy from a dream. He called for the police to accompany her out of the airport and they arrived in minutes.

Johanna didn't put up a fight with the police, in fact, she felt safe in the back seat of the police car, especially after discovering the officer who was driving was fluent in English. The police officer told Johanna he would drive her to the Western police station where she could gather her thoughts and talk to him about her visit to Hong Kong. As they traveled into the city, Johanna closed her burning eyes and drifted off to sleep.

The boy came to her again while she briefly napped in the police car. He was older than in the last dream, but he was so far away that she could only see a faint outline of a now taller boy.

"*Wan Chai* is where you will find me, *Wan Chai* is where the truth lives," the boy shouted.

"Wh-an Ch-eye?" she responded, but she was no longer sleeping, and still in the back of the car. The officer driving asked Johanna if she was going to the *Wan Chai* neighborhood of Hong Kong. She responded with a fast "yes" hoping he would change course and take her there.

"Would you take me to *Wan Chai?*" she asked.

"I don't know, I am worried about you," he said in a genuinely caring tone.

"No, I'm...I'm fine, I'm here for a funeral and I haven't had much sleep lately," she reassured him.

"I just need to get to my hotel and get some rest." Johanna gathered as much energy as she could to sound as rational as possible.

"Which hotel, the 88 or the Novotel, or..." Johanna cut off the police officer and hurriedly answered, "...the 88."

"If I take you to the 88, do you promise to get some rest and stay out of trouble?" he said in both a caring and firm tone.

"Oh yes, of course, I just need a hot shower and some rest," she responded, as meekly as possible.

The car drove away as Johanna stood there, in front of a hotel where she had no reservation, with a blank stare on her face. It was beautifully situated on the water, which always made Johanna feel calmer, and more connected to the *real* world than she normally felt. She wasn't sure what to do, the boy wasn't speaking to her while she was awake and the gravity of what she had just done was sinking in as the adrenaline began to wear off from the travel. She turned and walked into the hotel and used the only credit card that hadn't reached its limit to rent a room for the night. Johanna was never so grateful to feel the softness of a pillow in all of her life. She needed no assistance falling asleep; it was the first deep sleep she had in over a decade.

Johanna woke with an urgency. She looked at the small analog alarm clock in the corner and it read 2:07 am. Johanna slept almost nine hours in that hotel room and there was no dream, no boy, no direction for her to follow. She felt the need to leave the room almost as strongly as she felt the need to travel to Hong Kong the day before.

Johanna took a brief shower, brushed her teeth and changed into the only clothing she packed into her small backpack. She left the hotel, walking toward the row of restaurants and bars where people were ending their night and heading home.

As Johanna made her way toward the lights and the muffled sounds of people ending their evening, she saw the shadow of a man approaching her. The man was walking with labored breathing and a peculiar gait. Her heart started to pound violently in her chest and her mind immediately remembered the men in her dreams, the men who held her arms and laughed while she screamed for the boy she traveled all the way to Hong Kong to find.

Johanna ducked into an alley so the man could pass without seeing her and she waited until he was far enough ahead to be able to follow him. Her heart felt as though it would explode, there was a rage building inside of her, as though she was inherently angry with the stranger. What if he wasn't a stranger, what if he was someone from her past who hurt her? What if the men from her dreams were as real as the boy? She moved from the shadows of the alley and suddenly, the man stopped. Johanna knew she had been heard walking behind him.

Before she could react using reason, she grabbed a glass bottle from the street waste can and ran toward the man, striking him on the head with it. Johanna stood there, looking at the body that lay at her feet. She rifled through his pockets and took everything she could find: a wallet, a set of keys, a pack of cigarettes and a sealed envelope. Johanna panicked. She didn't want the man to identify her once he regained consciousness and called the police, so she had to think quickly about what to do. She looked to her left, to her right and back to her left again, where she spotted the broken bottle lying on the ground next to him. She plunged a shard of glass into his stomach, leaving the glass embedded in his flesh before running back in the direction of the 88. Leaving the sounds and lights of the emptying bars behind her, she held her hand over her mouth to muffle her cries.

Ameer

Ameer was gathering supplies for his fourth year as a primary school teacher in Islamabad. Over the last nine years, Ameer had done his very best to move on from the past. Since the age of twenty-five or so, he had started having dreams about his mother. She was always calling out for him, but he was never able to see her face. Ameer had forgotten what his mother's face looked like in person. There were photographs of her in the family home, but he lost the ability to see her in his mind's eye or remember the moments they shared together.

Ameer was a teacher that every one of his students adored. His students were young (fourth and fifth grade), and his classroom was still co-ed. The school was small, and it couldn't afford many of the modern amenities of wealthier schools, but it was in a safe and family-focused neighborhood of Islamabad. Ameer was proud and grateful to provide the same level of education to both male and female students in his school; he was very vocal in the pursuit of his country providing equal educational opportunities to girls.

The gender disparities in education in Pakistan was a difficult issue because many families could only afford to send their sons to school as the government began to charge fees for public education. Pakistan had long been plagued with a history of gender inequality where women were considered the property of their husbands as well as their sons. Ameer wanted to help change that, but it started to create a bit of animosity with his more conservative neighbors and family members, most notably, his father.

Ameer's father, Fawad, only respected a woman's place in the traditionally accepted spaces of the family. Fawad still believed that women were the property of their male family members and had little sympathy for a women's right to vote or receive a formal education. Ameer still lived with his father and chose to *agree to disagree* on this important issue, but this arrangement proved increasingly more difficult as he enveloped himself in his career and in politics. Ameer was an outspoken advocate for his students, which also meant speaking out against the archaic policies of the government relating to separating boys and girls in later grades, as well as keeping education from the poorest of students by charging fees.

"We need to talk, Ameer," said his father, Fawad, when Ameer arrived home from his work preparing for school. Ameer had just a few days before he was expecting students.

Ameer's relationship had been strained with his father for the last several years and each year they grew more and more distant.

"Sure...I don't have much time, though, I am due back at the school for sorting uniforms and textbooks," explained Ameer.

Fawad didn't wait a beat before responding, "Ameer, I want you leave your job at the school. It's creating strains in the family with your uncles and your actions are causing problems with their neighbors."

Ameer heard what Fawad said but he wasn't sure how to respond; he was still expected to at least *pretend* to obey his father even when he had every intention of ignoring his orders.

"You know I can't do that; I am obligated to follow through on my promise to my students and their families," replied Ameer, hoping that his father wouldn't be able to argue with the same logic that was being presented to him to resign.

"You remind me so much of your mother," said Fawad, not in a tone of a somber memory, but of anger and frustration.

"Please don't bring her into this, I can barely even remember her any longer," Ameer responded sternly, which caught him a bit off guard, to have spoken to his father in that way.

"I will bring her into *this* if I want and you will listen." Fawad's voice became louder and deeper, signaling an argument that Ameer had no interest in having at the moment.

Ameer wanted to diffuse the situation, narrowed his eyes and with a deep breath said, "I will see what I can do and inquire with the headmaster, tonight."

"You are headed for problems with your ideologies, we are a family of tradition," said Fawad in a deep quiet voice. He continued to speak with a look that Ameer last saw the day his mother disappeared. "Your mother had problems with these ideas as well; she would've been better served if she had just done what I told her to do."

Ameer felt his pulse begin to race as his father's eyes locked with his. Ameer was not interested in a confrontation with his father. He didn't feel as though his father was intellectually equal and had little respect for those that kept the archaic belief that women were somehow inferior. Ameer trusted women more than men; he believed women rarely had ulterior motives. Men abducted girls and young women and sold them to traffickers, men with the beliefs his father and his uncles held.

"Well, I am going to be late if I don't get going," Ameer stated as he attempted to end the uncomfortable situation.

Fawad didn't respond to Ameer, just simply kept staring into Ameer's eyes as though he was trying to intimidate him. Ameer's returned stares felt necessary as he wasn't sure what his father was going to say or do next.

"You better get going," Fawad coldly remarked, not moving his eyes away from Ameer's.

Ameer turned and walked away. He knew it was time to leave his father's house if he wanted to live his life without the fear of his father and his conservative extended family. Ameer was passionate about women's rights and equality and he had never been very close to his father, and since his mother's disappearance, he'd grown further and further from him.

Ameer left the house and did his best to put the conversation with his father behind him, for now. School was about to start for the year, and he had many things to do over the next few days. Ameer decided to try to avoid his father at all costs until he arranged for a new place to live. Little did he know, leaving his father's home would happen much sooner than he ever expected.

When Ameer arrived at school, he noticed someone had delivered a large white envelope to his classroom. The envelope had no return address on it and must have been delivered in the short time since he left the school, less than an hour ago. Ameer looked around his classroom before picking up the envelope to ensure that he was alone, and slowly opened it.

Inside were several large photographs and a typed letter. The photographs were images of a woman who looked troubled. She was wearing tattered clothing, her face was clean of makeup, and her hair was piled on top of her head in an untidy nest. Her eyes were swollen as though she had been crying and she looked like she was in distress. Her mouth was open in the pictures as if she was calling out to someone. She was clearly in an airport, but Ameer couldn't recognize which airport. After he quickly reviewed the pictures, realizing he didn't recognize the woman in them, he picked up the letter. It read:

> *Dear Ameer,*
> *I hope this letter finds you quickly. I have been suffering for many years with the guilt of what I am about to tell you and due to recent discoveries, it is time that you learned the truth about the disappearance of your mother, over twenty years ago.*
> *Azra, your mother, was abducted by a South African gang, the Clever Kids, when you were just a boy. She, and other young women and girls, were smuggled from Pakistan to the Nyanga township of South Africa. Your mother had not been seen in all these years, by anyone that knew her, until these pictures were taken as she was being escorted out of the Hong Kong International Airport*

for making a hysterical scene, only a few short
days ago.

It seems your mother is unwell, which is
understandable due to what she must have en-
dured as a trafficked woman.

The most painful part of this confession is
what I have yet to tell you, that your father
(and your uncles) sold your mother to the gang
for four million rupees. I tried to stop the
trade from happening, but I was told to mind
my place. I was threatened that I, too, would
be sold to the gang if I interfered and I haven't
been brave enough to come forward until now.

Please forgive me and go to her before it is
too late. Your mother is alive and needs your
help.

-A Loved One

Ameer dropped the envelope, the pictures, and the letter
without noticing them falling from his fingers and burst
into tears. The emotions running through his mind were
a mixture of complete sadness and a hesitant joy that his
mother was still alive. He had to go to her, tonight. She
was depending on him and he needed to right the wrongs
of his father, and his uncles, so many years ago.

Ameer picked up the photos from the floor and
studied his mother's face. He had her soft features and
even though she looked tired and scared, to him, she
was absolutely beautiful. He repeated the name he had
almost forgotten, Azra, while he looked in amazement at

her face. The memories came rushing back to him, hearing her sing while she cleaned their house, feeling her hair as she held him close at home and smelling her perfume while she prepared for her day. By this time, the tears were streaming from his eyes and pattering on the large, black-and-white photos he was holding. Nothing would be the same for Ameer now that he had made this discovery.

Clayton

Clayton completed culinary school six years ago and worked as an apprentice for several well-known Australian chefs in Sydney, Melbourne, and Brisbane before working his way up to sous chef at a busy restaurant in the Surrey Hills area of Sydney. Clayton's father's culinary skill was well-known by many in the industry and helped him get his foot in the door despite not graduating from a prestigious, and expensive, private culinary institution.

"Ah, Jim and I used to raise some hell back in Brisbane," and "Jimmy couldn't keep wandering eyes away from the hostess staff," and other similar comments would remind Clayton of the father he only knew for the first early years of his life.

Clayton was proud to have a father like Jim, but he couldn't change the past and he couldn't pretend that his father had much influence over his life. Clayton's career and talents as a chef wouldn't be a product of his father's warm fatherly guidance with knife skills or clever insider tips on how to properly prepare a chicken. Clayton would have to rely on his training and tenacity to better his own life. He was drawn to be a chef to honor his father, but that was nine years ago, and a lot had happened since his first day of culinary school. Clayton discovered his flair for cooking and excelled in molecular gastronomy, a cooking technique using chemicals to transform dishes into works of art. Clayton decided that it was time to go where the industry was always evolving and where he would have countless opportunities to work and sample cuisine from anywhere in the world; he decided to move to New York City.

Coincidentally, the day Clayton chose to move to New York, was the same date he started culinary school several years ago, August 8th. That small detail, or so he thought, made Clayton feel as though the universe was trying to tell him that he was making the right decision.

"Mum, I hope you're going to be able to get along without me," he said to his mother with a half-mouthed smile.

"I know that I'll be saving enough money on food to retire early!" she joked and gave him a forceful hug that he didn't expect, slightly knocking the wind out of him.

"Jesus, you been lifting weights?" he joked.

His mother started crying while keeping her embrace strong and soaking the side of his face and shoulder with her tears. "Don't forget about your only mother when you become a famous chef," she spoke lightly through her tears.

"I love you, mum," Clayton responded just as softly as the emotion caught up to him and he felt the lump in his throat grow.

It was almost dawn when Clayton started his journey to New York with a mixed feeling of excitement and fear. All that stood between him and his new life was a twenty-two-hour flight, (with a connection in Dallas) but he didn't mind. It would give him time to get the sleep he was too anxious to get over the last few days. As the plane climbed to cruising altitude, Clayton's eyelids began to close, and he slowly drifted into a deep and comfortable sleep.

Clayton's head fell to his left shoulder, his breath slowed and under his eyelids, his eyes rapidly twitched. He was transported to a serene view of far-off mountains, clear blue sky and warm, bright sunshine. Clayton turned around to see an old house; its bleakness was exaggerated by the beauty that surrounded it. Just as he was noticing the house, he could see a child in an upstairs window looking out at him. She was crying, and she was trying to say something to him. He waved to her, signaling that he couldn't hear what she was saying, but she kept yelling to him.

Clayton ran to the door of the house and noticed that it was already slightly open. He stepped inside and was immediately struck by an unexpected temperature change. The house was so cold that he could see his breath and there was a light frost covering the floors and a small couch, the only piece of furniture in the front room.

He shouted, "Hello? Little girl?"

There was no answer, but there was a creak in the floor upstairs. Clayton climbed the stairs to the second floor where he found a hallway and four closed doors within it. He walked to the door of the room where he saw the little girl and slowly opened it. The room was completely empty but even colder than the downstairs front room. The floor, the ceiling, and the window were completely encased in frost and Clayton shivered while slowly entering the room. The closet in the room was completely frosted over, just like the rest of the room, but Clayton wanted to check to see if the little girl was hiding inside. He walked over and made an attempt to open the door, but it wouldn't budge. Clayton tried again, but this time he gave the door a shove with his shoulder to break any ice that may be preventing it from opening and pulled the door open.

There was no frost inside the closet, instead, there were a child's drawings hanging on the walls and a pillow on top of a thin blanket folded in the corner. On the pillow was a piece of paper with a child's writing on it. It read, "I'm waiting."

Clayton was startled awake by a flight attendant asking him to return his seat to the upright position and prepare for landing. "Are we heading back to the airport?" he asked in a groggy, confused tone.

"No, sir, we are about to arrive in Dallas," responded the flight attendant, matter-of-factly.

Clayton was disoriented and still trying to comprehend how he had slept for nineteen hours. He saw that his tray table was down, a half-eaten cookie and cold cup of coffee was sitting in front of him. He also noticed his notepad sitting in his lap and an uncapped pen had fallen between his thighs.

"Sir, you'll also have to place your tray table in the locked position," the attendant reminded him.

As she walked away, Clayton picked up his notepad, and went for the cookie and coffee to raise the tray, when he saw he had written something on the paper. He brought the notepad closer to his face to read what was written. In his own handwriting, he read, "I'm waiting."

"I'm waiting?" Clayton whispered to himself, confused.

CHAPTER 4 – REVELATION
AND SACRIFICE

Ellen

"What are you waiting for?" Ellen heard a muffled, indistinguishable voice.

"WHAT. ARE. YOU. WAITING. FOR?" Mrs. Donovan's voice became tragically clear. She sharply questioned the sleeping girl as she stared down at Ellen. "The rules, Ellen, the rules are that you are downstairs and ready for breakfast at 4:30 am. Are you waiting for a personal invitation?" she snapped.

It was four-thirty in the morning, and it was also Ellen's birthday, August 8th.

The upstairs hallway light was on, and the door to Ellen's bedroom was open, making Mrs. Donovan's face and body just a black silhouette, which startled her. Ellen's bedroom was completely empty, with the exception of her closet which contained only a blanket, a pillow, and a few of her drawings. This was where Ellen was directed to sleep and where she spent the majority of her time when she wasn't cleaning, being *educated,* or tending the farm that the Donovans were working on converting to a place of worship. Ellen was given the responsibilities

of keeping the grounds looking presentable as the Donovans devoted most of their time designing and building
their new church. The farm hadn't seen real farm equipment or a real farm animal since the "family" moved in
several months ago.

Roger and Mary Donovan were Puritans.

"There are many misconceptions about our religion. Scarlett letters, burning witches and pilgrim cos-
tumes are no part of what you will be taught," Mrs. Donovan explained calmly.

"The Puritans lived according to the scriptures, no
more, no less, and we believe in adopting their simple
principles to restore order," Mr. Donovan further elabor-
ated.

The Donovans didn't celebrate birthdays as "that
would show an ungratefulness for God, as individual-
ity holds no value in Puritanism." This was a regularly
stated edict in the house whenever Ellen felt fear, didn't
like the taste of something she was provided for food,
wanted to rest from a long morning of chores, or needed
medicine for a cold or injury.

"We chose you, to *mold you*," she continued. "We
knew of your troubles and realized you were marked,
marked to live a tragic life because you are inherently
wicked," she said point-blank to Ellen, a child, without
the slightest movement on her cold face.

Mrs. Donovan opened her mouth just enough to
allow for the smallest, most biting sound, to ask, "Do you

understand that about yourself?"

A cold silence fell upon the room.

Ellen looked like she had seen a ghost and took a few shallow breaths before answering her, "I do, Mother."

"Good," Mrs. Donovan responded, narrowing her eyes with suspicion. "That is an important part of your conditioning."

Ellen was very cunning for her young age. Though she was confused and heartbroken with the loss of the only person she ever knew as "family," it only took her a few moments to know how to respond to that awful question.

As time passed with the Donovans, Ellen, now ten-years-old, was starting to believe what they were telling her. The Donovans *believed* what they were telling her, they *believed* they had entered a covenant with God. They *believed* modern American society had moved too far from the scriptures.

The barn behind the house was quickly being modified to hold a congregation as well as provide an altar for the minister, Mr. Donovan. Ellen had mostly been working in the barn over the last few days, clearing the excess pieces of lumber, sweeping up sawdust and sanding the new pews that had been installed.

Today, Ellen's hands were raw and sore from the never-ending task of sanding with just a small, hand-sized block of sandpaper. The work was tedious, but Ellen could escape into her own thoughts as she kept to herself and stayed away from the attention of the Donovans. They had been focused on nothing other than the completion of the church to ready it for the planned opening services on Sunday.

The couple had been attempting to indoctrinate Ellen into their religious beliefs ever since the family arrived in Colorado. The teachings of their church were foreign to Ellen; she had very little education in any formal religious texts or "scriptures." The Donovans gave Ellen a book soon after moving to the farm and told her to study it to prepare for the opening of the new church. The Donovans called it *The Geneva Bible* and they said it was the only *true* Bible.

Sunday arrived and Ellen was exhausted. She wasn't exactly sure how to feel about the completion of the church. The idea of something new was appealing to her, but there were hesitations about what was next in her transition to becoming a Puritan. Ellen was reading through her Bible, but none of it was making much sense, so the words simply passed by her eyes in an exercise of collecting completed pages and doing what she was told. There was a worry growing inside of her and she knew the education of her new arrangement with God was going to be starting, now that the right environment was standing in its plain, unassuming structure behind a plain, unassuming house.

Several families had followed mother and father Donovan to Colorado, and they also managed to amass a small congregation since arriving on the farm. Soon after dawn, cars began arriving and parking single file next to the barn. Mrs. Donovan was preparing for service in the house, while Mr. Donovan was showing the visitors the new church, generating an excitement among the group as well as the hosts.

Ellen looked through the backdoor window and noticed that all of the new arrivals were wearing very similar clothing. The women and girls were in heavy, solid color dresses and the men were in heavy, solid color suits, white shirts and black ties. The plainness of their dress wouldn't have been as obvious with everyone on their own, but with the full congregation all dressed so plainly, the scene reminded Ellen of the funeral she attended for her father several years ago. That memory made Ellen very introspective and still, that is, until she was interrupted by the heavy clack of Mother's shoes.

"This is for you." She handed Ellen a kelly-green, wool, shin-length dress. "This is what you will wear for Wednesday, Friday and Sunday services. This is your service dress," she instructed Ellen.

Mother handed Ellen another plain, white, and much lighter dress. "This is your day dress, for education." She continued while Ellen held the two dresses out in front of her, trying not to show any reaction to their appearance, "You will continue to wear your chore clothes and your night clothes, as usual."

"Do you understand, Ellen?" she impatiently

asked.

"I do, Mother," responded Ellen.

Mother sharply ordered, "Now go change, service is soon to begin."

Ameer

Ameer arrived in Hong Kong much like his mother, frantic, calling for someone who was not there. He was walking through the airport with an urgency but had no real place to go. All he knew, was his mother was *somewhere* in or around Hong Kong.

Ameer studied Mandarin during his university studies as part of his training to be a teacher, his original plan was to teach English to Chinese students due to the issues surrounding education in Pakistan. His primary and secondary education focused heavily on learning English and it seemed like a good opportunity to see a different part of the world. Never, did Ameer expect to be immersed and practicing his foreign language skills while on a wild-goose-chase to find the mother he thought was dead.

He opened his shoulder bag and removed pictures that were left for him to discover in his classroom. He shuffled through them until he noticed he was standing in front of the same exit door where his mother had been photographed. He showed the picture to several of the guards, asking if they remembered seeing the woman in the photograph when one of them pointed out that *he* was in the photograph. He told Ameer the woman was taken into police custody, from the Western police station, and to inquire with them on her whereabouts. Ameer thanked the man and immediately got into a cab.

Ameer arrived at the Western police station and inquired about his mother, showing the pictures to several officers.

"We don't usually deal with calls from the airport; did you inquire within the Airport police station?" asked the first officer he spoke to, as she was making her way out of the station.

"I was told that since she was not really a threat, she was brought here to calm down to be removed from the place that seemed to be upsetting her," replied Ameer.

He made his way through a few more officers, when he heard a man speaking about how busy the airport had been these last few days. "People have been in rare form lately; just last week we had to chase a drunk lady through terminal one," the man chuckled as he spoke.

"Excuse me, sir, would you have happened to come across this woman?" he asked, holding up the clearest photo of his mother's face to the officer.

"Well, yes, I remember this woman quite well. She was in a hurry and looked a bit...*lost*," the officer vividly recalled his interaction with Johanna. "Why, do you know her?"

"She's my mother," answered Ameer.

"She asked to be dropped at the Wenchai 88 Hotel, not too far from here," said the officer. "It's just a few minutes by taxi, east on route four."

"I appreciate it," Ameer hurriedly responded as he raced out of the police station.

Johanna

Johanna hadn't really slept in five days. She had periods of dozing off, but when she actually attempted to sleep, all she could think about was that man lying in the street, bleeding. Is this what she had become, someone so out of touch with reality that she could *murder* someone so coldly?

Johanna couldn't stay in the room at the 88. She needed to leave, she needed to get away from Hong Kong, from South Africa, from India or Pakistan, from anywhere that anyone would know or recognize her, and disappear once again.

She looked through her jacket pockets to find the wallet of the stranger she attacked. In the wallet were two credit cards and three thousand Hong Kong dollars, which could definitely get her somewhere, she thought. She looked at the resident identity card in the wallet, the man's name was Li Qiang Liu, from Beijing. She wondered who this man was and who would be missing him.

"Oh, right," she said to herself, discovering the letter she hastily took from the man as he lay unconscious and bleeding.

The letter was crumpled and still inside its once tidy, mostly clean envelope, except for a small smudge of blood near one of the back corners. The sight of the blood made Johanna feel nauseous with guilt. Slowly, she opened the envelope and unfolded the crisp paper, but the letter was written in Mandarin, a language she didn't know. She tucked the envelope back into her jacket pocket and packed up her belongings, readying herself to leave the hotel and Hong Kong. She made her way to the lobby and asked the young woman at the front desk if she knew English. The young woman said, "Yes, fairly well."

"Could you interpret a letter for me, and write down what it says while I use the computer over there?"

"Oh, sure, of course," said the young woman, looking slightly uncomfortable with the request.

Johanna gave the letter to the young woman and made her way to the computer. She pulled the stolen wallet from her jacket pocket and selected the first visible credit card. She needed to go somewhere no one would know her, where it would be unlikely that anyone would ever find her.

"New York!" she shouted, as a few of the hotel guests gave her a glance. Johanna assumed with so many people of all races and colors, that she would easily be hidden amongst the diversity of the big city.

Johanna booked a flight to New York, with a layover in Los Angeles that would leave Hong Kong International Airport in a little under two hours. The young woman approached Johanna and told her the letter wasn't really making sense, and she wondered if her English was not as good as it used to be, after all. She handed Johanna the letter, and the translation, and watched her turn around and walk toward the door of the hotel. The letter was puzzling to the young woman who wasn't really sure how to come to terms with what she just read. Was the letter part of a game in which the woman was involved, or perhaps a joke someone was playing on her?

Johanna exited the hotel, walked away from the valet toward Thomson Road, and noticed a cab pulling up on the opposite side of the street. A man got out of the cab, holding a large photograph and shouting to her. She was startled, wondering why the man was calling to her, shouting, "Azra." Who or what was Azra? Did she know the man calling after her? She instinctually turned and started running away from him as he entered the street.

Ameer was running across the street as Johanna was trying to escape him, moving quickly in the other direction. Just then, the sharp, screeching sound of tires and the smell of burning brakes from a city bus, came barreling toward his, by comparison to the oncoming bus, insignificant body.

Ameer was struck so violently by the bus, that he was thrown into a parked car where his crooked, broken body lay lifeless, propped up against the driver-side door of the car. His eyes were wide open, as if he was looking at the picture that was still firmly held in his fist. Johanna was brought to her knees by what she just witnessed and as strangers and bus passengers ran to the man, she managed to get to her feet and run away from the accident and the hotel.

Ellen

Ellen was being led into the church by Mother and Father, in her kelly-green dress, walking through the middle of the congregation as everyone's eyes were locked on her. She was confused, why did it seem as though she was on display for everyone to see? She was led to the altar and turned around to face the congregation. Ellen noticed some women were praying, children were shielding their faces with their hands and others were watching without any emotion. Mother grabbed her right arm and Father held her left, spreading her arms, like she was flying, with palms facing the congregation.

Mother and Father both pulled a small, ornate knife from each of their garments and recited, in unison, "Today, we spill the blood of the wicked, to kill the beast that dwells within, to end one life so that another may thrive."

They firmly grasped Ellen's small wrists so tightly that her hands were turning a purplish red as they raised their knives to the sky.

In one motion and at exactly the same time, both knives sliced into Ellen's wrists, causing the congregation to gasp and even more of them began to pray. There was a small trickle of blood with the immediate cut, but a split second later, the crimson liquid began to jet out of her wrists like a small fountain and coat the floor of the altar in front of them.

Ellen screamed in pain and confusion as the blood, and life, drained from her body. She thrashed in an attempt to free herself from the grasp of her "parents" and couldn't understand why no one was helping her. Mother and Father shouted again in unison:

"This child is wicked."

"Kill the beast so that she may live pure."

"Drain the evil blood from her wicked heart."

Ellen was no longer able to struggle as she was too weak from losing so much blood. She lost consciousness and slumped to the floor in her kelly-green dress, which stood out so vividly now that it was surrounded by a large pool of her dark red blood.

CHAPTER 5 – MOVEMENT

Sarah

After her fainting incident, nine years ago, at the annual family reunion, things went downhill very quickly for Sarah. Her parents, not the most affectionate people, became frustrated with her unresponsiveness to treatment of any kind, and started to look toward a more "permanent" solution as she approached her teenage years.

"I am afraid of what will happen to you if we aren't here twenty-four hours a day."

"Will we come home to a dead daughter this week?"

"What are YOU doing today to help yourself?" and other similar comments were regular parts of her interactions with her parents.

Sarah didn't know how to respond to these interrogations; she was completely blind-sided by her mood swings and just couldn't control them. As she got older, the feelings dramatically intensified and morphed into other issues in addition to the mood swings. At first, the voices came to her only in her dreams which she began documenting in her journal entries.

After a few years, she began hearing commentary in her head, voices that weren't her own inner voice but which seemed like the voices in her dreams. These voices were now coming to her while she was awake.

Sarah felt she was a spectator in other people's lives, people that had no idea she was watching. The visions she had in her dreams were making their way into Sarah's consciousness, during her waking hours. These were short glimpses, and she would usually see the same people, but only sporadically.

There was one person, though, that began speaking directly to Sarah. The running, fearful woman began to visit her often, sometimes daily. She told her parents about this woman, older than she, named Azra, who was very troubled and was running from something. She would often have conversations with Azra, asking her what she was running from and she would tell Sarah that she didn't really know why she was running, at all. Sarah told her she would help her, and Azra made Sarah commit to keeping that promise.

One Saturday afternoon, soon before her thirteenth birthday, Sarah's mother was on her way to return folded laundry to Sarah's bedroom, and heard her carrying on a conversation with someone else, yet she and Sarah were the only two people home that day. Sarah's mother heard her daughter speak in her own, soft, feminine voice, but responded to herself in a much deeper, older voice.

"Sarah, who are you talking to up here?" she asked, after catching her completely off-guard.

"You scared me! Were you listening to me talking to Azra, mom?" Sarah responded, feeling slightly embarrassed, but also relieved she didn't have to hide Azra from her anymore.

"Well, I heard you talking to someone, and I am more relieved that you are talking to yourself than a mass murderer," her mother tried to make the situation less awkward than she thought it was.

Later that evening, once Sarah's father came home from spending the day on his neighbor's speed boat, the couple decided to have a conversation with their daughter about the voices that she had been hearing.

"Sarah, we would like to try to understand your relationship with the woman that you have been speaking to in your room, I believe her name is, Azure?" her mother said to her.

"It's Azra," Sarah quickly corrected her mother.

"Regardless of her name, we think this may be moving in a direction your mother and I are uncomfortable heading in right now with you," her father firmly stated.

"What do you mean?" Sarah immediately questioned what was behind this conversation.

"Your mother and I have been discussing the *best* way to help you, and we believe we found the answer," her father said, handing her a brochure for a residential, in-patient psychiatric institution.

Sarah was sent to Syracuse, New York, when she was thirteen years old, where she was close enough to visit yet far enough away for her parents to get on with their lives with as few interruptions from their daughter's issues, as possible. Sarah lived in a facility with other young women who were experiencing mental health and behavioral issues. The facility was called, "Progressions." Sarah was comfortable in her new home, with the exception of her lack of privacy to be able to speak to Azra as freely as she was able to in her parents' home in Baltimore.

Azra was a subject that Sarah never brought up to her counselors, as she didn't want them to try and take her away, even if she was just a "construct of a disorder." She found peace in Azra, as if they were living similar lives. Sarah felt a connection to the her, and Azra told Sarah they were part of a special group of people that would one day be tested. Sarah realized these conversations were far too important to share with anyone else and Azra also requested she keep their talks to herself. Sarah promised, of course, and trusted her only confidant to tell her what she needed to know of this *special* group of people.

As the years passed by, Sarah grew into a young woman, becoming more comfortable and self-aware than ever before. Her discussions with Azra were frequent, and she was excelling in her academic studies while living at Progressions. Sarah's mood swings, from jubilation to despair, were almost completely gone from her life as long as she maintained communication with Azra. Several times, when Azra would be silent for extended periods, Sarah would lapse into depression and view the world completely differently than the day before, but as soon as her *internal companion* would return, she would also return to the person she was comfortable being.

Sarah's time at Progressions never produced any true or notable friendships with the others also staying at the facility. Her counselors often voiced their concerns that she wasn't acclimating to the group, but slowly their concerns waned as they saw Sarah thriving, even though she was alone most of the time. Sarah didn't get along well with the other residents and didn't feel that any of them were struggling with her same problems. She didn't consider Azra a problem, in fact, she saw her as a solution to her earlier issues as someone suffering with bipolar disorder.

As time passed, Sarah lived full-time at Progressions, but was able to visit her parents in Baltimore. These visits would take Sarah back to a place of discomfort and sadness. Her mother would be more and more impatient with her, as if she had moved on from being a parent now that Sarah was no longer depending on her for basic survival. Sarah's father was never really much of a presence in her life, and he continued to stay on the sidelines. Her visits home became less and less prevalent as she grew closer to her eighteenth birthday.

Eventually, Sarah stopped going back to her parents' house, even during major holidays when many of the residents left, with the exception of those who were too sick to travel. She would celebrate Christmas and Thanksgiving with families that would come to the facility as well as the staff that acted like parents, more than her real parents ever had.

Sarah's parents, with the exception of paying the monthly fee for Progressions, stopped being any part of her life, at all, by the age of seventeen. She was on her own now, she thought, and she was free to live with Azra safely tucked behind her eyes, guiding her through her everyday decisions and taking over her personality almost completely. Soon, Azra would be Sarah, and Sarah would be Azra.

At twenty-years old, Sarah planned on leaving Progressions. The institution offered her a counselor position within the facility to be in charge of organizing daily group meetings as well as all community life within the facility. Sarah politely declined the offer and explained she needed to move beyond this stage in her life. She was also in a hurry to begin her life again, as Azra, a woman Sarah admired and who freed her of the problems she had faced most of her young life. Sarah decided she was going to move to a place where she could begin her new life without shame, or her internal struggles. Sarah was going to move to New York City as Azra.

Johanna

Johanna boarded her flight to New York City, with only a few minutes to spare. The flight attendant's greeting and safety presentation mentioned the flying time to her connection in Los Angeles was a little over twelve hours which would, hopefully, provide Johanna with enough time to relax and catch her breath from the last week of her life. She was haunted by the look on the young man's face when he was struck by the bus in front of the 88 Hotel. He seemed to have known her but was calling out for someone else, someone named Azra.

Johanna had developed an instinctual fear of men since she lost her memory, and this young man triggered that instinct as he ran toward her with such strong intention. Now that she reflected on what happened, she felt a strong sense of guilt about the accident. "If he is dead, I am partly to blame," Johanna whispered to herself as she tried to settle into her seat, looking out the window and watching Hong Kong slowly fade out of sight. She breathed a sigh of relief as she climbed in altitude but, at the same time, felt the grounding weight of two lives on her shoulders. Johanna didn't know if these men were dead, but she was almost certain that they were, and if so, she had their blood on her hands.

Johanna needed to try to put the incidents with the shadowy stranger and the young man behind her and focus on her arrival in New York, as a way of moving on from everything in her past. She never found the boy she was chasing to Hong Kong, and she was still in the dark about her life before the hospital stay in South Africa. Perhaps the boy would come to Johanna again, in her sleep and give her further instructions. No matter what was to happen, Johanna vowed to let the last week of her life stay buried in the past with her lost memory.

Just as she was reflecting on her harrowing ordeal in Hong Kong, Johanna remembered the letter and the translation provided by the young woman from the hotel that was still in her pocket. Although it violated the pact she just made with herself, she still wanted to know what was contained in the letter.

She pulled the now crumpled pieces of paper from her pocket and opened the original letter, written in Mandarin, and studied the symbols and the artistry of the letters. It was beautifully simple but elegantly written. Even though she didn't understand the language, she could comprehend its sincerity. She honored the original letter writer in her thoughts, without ever knowing him, and wondered if the man she attacked received this letter, had written this letter, or was delivering this letter. She would never know, but she needed to honor the man she had possibly killed, she thought, and reading the letter would be part of that gesture. After these thoughts rushed through her mind, she decided to read the translation:

Dear Fellow Original,

I am sure that you are getting along with life much as I was before I received a letter very similar to this one. Before I go on further, I would like to tell you that I, too, lived a life of sadness and tragedy through most of my journey on Earth.

You are a part of a long line of people called Originals, chosen to protect the future of humankind. After the way humans have treated you, thus far in your life, I am sure you may need further explanation, so I will provide that to you.

I received a letter from the Original before me as well, only it had come very late in my life. This letter is much more effective when it is delivered as early in the next Original's life as possible, so that it can help to end the pain you, and others, have felt.

You begin a process called a Legacy, in which you are the first in your line of succession of other chosen humans...

"Sorry, I did not get to finish the translation, I have a customer!" was written at the bottom of the paper on which the woman from the hotel had written the translation.

"Protect the future of humankind?" Johanna repeated, trying to understand what, exactly, she just read.

The original letter was much longer than the translation that was provided by the woman from the hotel, and Johanna knew there was most likely an explanation for the strange opening of the letter.

"Perhaps, I am the *Original*," Johanna whispered to herself and looked around to make sure no one heard her. She paused to think she may have taken the letter from its intended recipient before he had a chance to read the letter.

"But the letter describes someone who has lived a life of sadness and tragedy," Johanna said to herself. Surely, no one would argue things had never been easy for her, at least, for as long as she could remember, anyway.

Johanna sat there, in her seat on the plane to Los Angeles, wondering if she was meant to encounter that man in Hong Kong in order to retrieve this letter? She was tempted to ask someone on the plane to translate the rest, but she didn't want anyone else to know this secret, and she also didn't want anyone to trace this letter back to the man she left to die, alone, in an alley from a stab wound she inflicted. She would have to wait to translate the rest of the letter another way, after her arrival in New York City.

Johanna closed her eyes and tried to imagine a new life in a new city, where she could be anyone with almost any history. She would tell the new people that she met about her "normal life," her happy upbringing and her completely intentional move to New York for more opportunities. Johanna didn't have a plan for work or for any particular living arrangements, so that would all have to be worked out fairly quickly once she arrived in the city. She would try to get by on her disability payments for now and rent a room at a hostel or other inexpensive alternative to a hotel or apartment. For now, though, at this exact moment in time, Johanna was safe. Her mysterious abduction and sexual assault, her suicidal thoughts, her constant battles with her own mind, were all things that could wait for the twelve hours she had to be worry free.

CHAPTER 6 – ARRIVAL

Clayton

Clayton arrived at the JFK airport in New York City, where he took the AirTrain to the A Line, directly into Manhattan. He was headed to meet his new roommate, Scott, an American from Texas who was also a newly relocated chef, looking to make a name for himself in the city. As Clayton exited the subway, Scott was waiting for him on the platform and desperately trying to identify Clayton based on the one time the pair had video chatted. Scott had arrived in the city a little over a week ago and wanted to show Clayton the layout of the apartment and also pick which room he wanted as his own, during that initial chat.

Scott shouted to Clayton when he locked eyes with him, "Clayton, hey Clayton...CLAYTON!"

Scott was tall, blonde and tan and as quintessentially Texan as Clayton had always imagined an American Texan would be. His thick dialect almost seemed exaggerated, but made Clayton feel comforted in this new city with all these unfamiliar people coming at him from every direction. Scott's booming voice stood out at the subway station, and the charming drawl of Clayton's name was unmistakable.

Clayton waved at Scott and hurried over with his duffle bag weighing on half of his body, looking as though he had a pronounced limp.

"How was the flight?" Scott, still louder than anyone around him, asked as he embraced Clayton with an unexpected hug.

"Good, I think. I fell asleep for the entire trip, I must have been exhausted," he responded.

"Well, it's a good thing, I have a lot to show you and we need to get some things for the apartment," Scott said with more excitement in his voice than Clayton was expecting.

Clayton knew that Scott was much different from anyone he knew in Sydney, but he welcomed his positive energy to help him acclimate to this new place. Their apartment was in Washington Heights, a friendly and safe neighborhood within the borough of Manhattan, and a perfect location to be centrally located to all of the city's amenities and restaurants.

Just as the two new friends were about to make their way up to the apartment, located on the third floor of a converted brownstone, Clayton heard a man shouting and running toward him, "Ron, hey Ron! Is that you, Ron?"

"I'm sorry?" Clayton responded, "My name isn't Ron, it's Clayton."

"Wow, you look and sound just like someone I

haven't seen in twenty years, same accent and every-thing!" said the stranger.

"I guess what they say is true, we all have a dop-pelganger somewhere," Clayton nervously laughed while attempting to carry on casually with this unexpected conversation.

"You have a dad named Ron?" the man asked Clay-ton to help satisfy his amazement at the similarities be-tween his friend "Ron" and Clayton.

Clayton slowly glanced at the man with a defeated look on his face, not really wanting to discuss such a deeply personal issue with someone he didn't know.

"No, sorry, my dad's name is Jim...uh...James, and he passed away a long time ago," Clayton said in a quiet, somber voice.

"Oh, man, I'm sorry, didn't mean any disrespect," said the man with an obviously regretful tone.

"No worries," responded Clayton.

Clayton and Scott made their way into the build-ing and they climbed the narrow stairs to the third floor. It was August, and very humid in New York, and both men reached their apartment dripping with sweat due to the walk from the subway combined with climbing the stairs.

"All this concrete and glass retains heat, whew!" said Scott as he slid the key into the lock. "I thought Texas was hot," he clamored on as he wiggled the key until it eventually opened the door to the mostly empty apartment.

Clayton followed Scott into the stuffy apartment. Scott had brought in a few items that he purchased over the last few weeks: two chairs, a side table, some pots and pans, and other essentials like toothpaste and toilet paper. Clayton went to the room he had chosen to set down his heavy duffle bag. It was a very small room, but it was freshly painted a clean, new, white and the window was perfectly functional. The apartment was a promising start to this new life and Scott seemed like someone he could call a friend, but his excitement was stunted by the stranger outside, calling him "Ron."

Clayton tried to shake the feeling of sad nostalgia and made his way back to the living room.

"Welcome home," Scott turned and shouted to Clayton with both arms raised to the ceiling.

"Cheers," Clayton responded, still affected but trying not to let it show to his brand-new roommate.

Sarah

Sarah had been in New York for a few days, staying at a hostel in the Hell's Kitchen neighborhood of Manhattan. She needed a place to stay while she finalized arrangements to sublet an apartment from a couple traveling abroad for six months. Sarah wanted to make sure she would like New York before making any *major* commitments, and this seemed like a logical way to do that.

Azra has been absent ever since she arrived in New

York and Sarah was beginning to get worried. She had been talking to her daily before the move, and she hoped the change in environment wouldn't change her relationship with the only friend she ever had. Sarah's mind was calm and quiet when she spoke to Azra and she could feel tension and sadness creeping back to her, as if she was going through withdrawal from her presence.

It was early morning on Sarah's last day at the hostel and she was lying on her bed staring at the ceiling, soon after waking, thinking of Azra.

Sarah whispered to herself, "Azra, I really do miss you and I want to tell you about New York!"

She continued, "I need you. Without you, I am lost and afraid. I don't want to go back to the person I was before I met you."

"I am here, Sarah," Azra finally responded.

"Thank God you're back, where have you been?" questioned Sarah, with a noticeable tone of relief in her voice.

"I was speaking to you the entire time, Sarah; it is *you* that couldn't hear *me*," said Azra, impatiently.

"You were? I am so sorry, I would never have done that to you intentionally," explained Sarah.

"I know, Sarah. Now, tell me, how do you like the city?" inquired Azra.

"Oh, it is so overwhelming, which is why I needed to speak to you. Knowing that you are here with me changes everything," Sarah continued with tears welling in her eyes. "I don't want to live without you."

"You won't have to, Sarah, we are now part of one another, and I will never leave you," Azra softly reassured her.

Sarah quickly followed, "Thank you, I know I can always rely on you, and you can always rely on me, too!"

"I know," she said even softer and calmer than before. "Sarah, I do have a request for you, now that we are in a new place."

"Of course, anything," Sarah quickly responded.

"I would like you to begin using the name, Azra. I want the world to know who you *really* are," she said with a firmer tone.

Sarah hesitated for a second, knowing that this is all she had wanted since before she left for New York. "I would be honored."

Sarah jumped out of bed and packed the few things that she brought with her from Progressions and made her way downstairs from her room, for the last time.

"Checking out?" the young attendant from behind the front desk asked.

"Yes, thank you," she replied.

Sarah put her suitcase down and settled the bill with the attendant as a group of young men dressed in tuxedos exited the hostel.

"People love getting married in Central Park in summer," replied the attendant.

"I am sure," Sarah replied in agreement.

As the door closed behind the groom's party, a frazzled looking woman entered the lobby, smelling as if she had spent several days in the same clothing, without a shower, and stood behind Sarah while she signed her credit card receipt.

"Thank you for staying at the Hell's Kitchen Hostel, Sarah," the attendant kindly spoke.

"You're welcome, and thank you for the comfortable room," Sarah replied, and hesitated, before adding, "Oh, and you can call me, Azra."

Sarah took her exit as the woman behind her stared at her with a look of astonishment. The woman watched her walk through the door and down the sidewalk, out of sight. The woman hurried back to the desk and asked the young woman attendant, "What name did she say you could call her?"

"I think she said, *Azra?*" replied the attendant.

"That's what I thought," replied the woman.

She composed herself, without putting too much thought into what she just heard, for now.

"I would like to stay here for a month, if that is possible?" the woman asked of the young attendant, to which she replied,

"Of course! We have long-term guests visit New York quite often. What brings you to the city, and what is your name?"

"Well, I'm not really sure, but I think I am here to make some new friends, and my name is Johanna," she replied with a slight smirk on her face. She continued, "Would it be possible to take some extra towels to my room, I need a major spa day after these last few days of traveling."

The young woman giggled, "I know what you mean, traveling can be a dirty business." She continued, "Give me one moment and I will get them for you."

As the attendant left to get the extra towels, Johanna leaned over the desk to the read the ledger and get the name of the woman that was standing at the counter before her.

"Okay, Sarah Martin, we will meet again," Johanna quietly whispered to herself as she scribbled the name and phone number off the ledger and onto the paper she had in her pocket that contained the translation from Hong Kong.

"Here you are, will four towels be enough for you to get settled?" asked the young woman.

"Most definitely, thank you!" replied Johanna, as she gathered her things to take to her room.

Johanna made her way to the place she would be calling home for the month and sat on the chair next to the simple bed, with a deep and long-lasting exhale of relief. As the items in her hands fell to the floor of the room, Johanna broke down with a flood of emotion that was just too strong to fight. Here, she sat, and cried for herself, for the stranger she left in the alley, for the young man calling after her with the name, "Azra" and for the young woman she just encountered who called herself by that same, unusual name.

This was all too much for Johanna right now, after her long journey from Hong Kong to New York City, so she sprawled her tired, dirty limbs on the clean, twin bed in the room and, finally, rested her eyes. Johanna almost immediately lost consciousness while the noisy, busy city outside may as well have been a world away.

CHAPTER 7 – TOGETHER

Li Qiang

Li Qiang's body was found several hours after the attack in the alley where he was left by Johanna. The sun was beginning to rise, and an elderly couple was taking their, equally, elderly dog for a very slow and peaceful Sunday morning walk to the pier. As they walked through the alley short-cut to the bench where they sipped their coffee and enjoyed the cooler morning air, they noticed a large, unidentifiable pile of what looked like blankets or coats. As they approached the object, it became abundantly clear that it was a body, closer still, now a man. Closer still, they could see it was an unconscious man surrounded by a pool of his own, now mostly dried, blood.

The alley became a crime scene with detectives and officers collecting evidence and attempting to understand what happened to the unidentified man.

"The pockets of his pants are turned inside out, and he has no wallet, money, or identification on him," commented the officer who arrived first on the scene after the original call was received from the old couple.

"Looks like a standard mugging," responded the

detective, crouching down by Li Qiang's body.

Just then, the detective noticed the stab wound on his stomach as they rolled him onto his back to examine his entire body for injuries.

"Now, why would a mugger want to kill him?" the detective questioned himself while writing notes and asking the crime scene photographer to take photos of the stab wound.

"Could've put up a good fight, the mugger might have needed some time to run away," replied an officer standing with the detective.

"Yeah, true," said the detective, holding up the small piece of green, pointed glass he removed from the victim's belly. "Looks like the mugger was desperate, here, let's dust this for prints." The detective handed the shard of glass to the officer holding an evidence bag. There was an obvious fingerprint on the green glass from the bottle used to kill Li Qiang.

Sarah

Sarah made her way to the sublet where she would be staying for the next six months. The apartment was small, but very comfortable. The couple that lived in the apartment was obviously very artistic, with large and small paintings covering every empty space on the walls, making Sarah feel at-home and in an element of creativity and endless new possibilities. Sarah had a good feeling about this place, and she couldn't wait to make this city her own.

Sarah received a small income from her last few years at Progressions. She had been working as a liaison with the families of the residents of the facility by answering the phones during the day and directing family members on how to pay their monthly dues as well as educating them on visiting hours, updates on the care their residents received, and new policies that would impact them. She saved her earnings as her expenses were all paid by her parents. Sarah thought it was the least they could have done since they'd, essentially, disowned her now that she was an adult and old enough to take care of herself.

Sarah's parents had no idea their daughter left Progressions and, as requested by Sarah, the facility did not release any information related to her discharge. One day, though, their monthly payment was returned, and a letter followed, that simply stated:

> *Dear Mr. and Mrs. Martin,*
>
> *We appreciate the opportunity to provide your daughter, Sarah Martin, with quality care for the last six years. Sarah's behavior has greatly improved, and she will no longer require your monthly contribution.*
>
> *We here at Progressions wish you, and your family, all the best.*
> *Samuel Groff*
> *Director of Resident Services*
> *Progressions Institute of Psychological and Behavioral Health*

Mr. and Mrs. Martin received the letter a few days after Sarah arrived in New York. As Sarah was settling into her new home, she received a phone call from her father. She looked at the caller ID on her phone and wasn't sure what she wanted to do. If she answered the call, she would need to explain to her father where she was as well as why she never informed him of her departure from Progressions. Sarah wasn't ready to have that conversation with her father, so she let the phone ring and go to voicemail. After a few minutes, she looked at her phone, noticing her father never left a message.

Surprisingly, Sarah wasn't really all that upset her father decided not to leave a voicemail. She had found a new strength in her alternative identity. No longer was she weighed down by grief and mood swings. No longer was she feeling the weight of the entire human race on her shoulders, as it felt for so many years of her young life. Azra became the sanctuary from all of the pain and the confusion, and Sarah became more and more dependent on this relationship, so much that she slowly started to forget herself.

After her first day of exploring her new neighborhood, only a few short blocks from Central Park, Sarah realized just how lucky she was in this apartment as she would never have been able to afford this apartment, in this location, on her own. She couldn't believe just how easily everything was falling into place for her. She had a new name, a new apartment, and a new outlook on life. Sarah settled in for the first night of the rest of her life, in one of the most comfortable beds she could remember. As thoughts of contentment entered her mind, she slowly drifted off, into a deep sleep.

Through the mist, Sarah could see that she was approaching a woman, a woman that was screaming while standing over a man on the ground. The man was groaning in pain and the woman was frantically searching for something, screaming and obviously confused. Sarah watched the woman pick up a piece of glass from a broken beer bottle nearby, and slowly walk toward the man as she cried. The woman crouched down to the man and forced the shard of glass into his stomach while turning her head, so that she wouldn't see what she was doing. The woman ran away from the scene of the crime, leaving Sarah by herself with the bleeding man, who was now unconscious and no longer groaning.

Sarah looked at the man, who now seemed so peaceful, and started to kneel closer to his body. Just as she crouched down, she looked at her hands, and they were grasping the shard of glass that was lodged in the man's stomach. She immediately released the glass and held her hands dripping with the man's blood in front of her face. She stood up and ran away from him, stopping once she approached a hotel appearing from the dense fog. Sarah was covered in the man's blood, not only on her hands, but now completely coating her clothing and parts of her arms and legs.

The hotel was across the street from where she was standing, and she could see a man just a few feet from her, shouting to someone near the hotel; it was the woman that she saw earlier in the alley. The woman turned and ran from the man as he entered the street to chase after her. Just as he entered the street, Sarah heard the screeching of tires and watched the man and a bus come into contact with one another. Right before he was thrown from his feet, from the impact, Sarah heard the man shout, "Azra," which surprised her so much that it thrust her to a seated position in her bed, waking her from the sleep that had started so peacefully.

"Azra, are you there?" Sarah called.

"I just had the most terrifying dream and I need you," she pleaded to her alter-ego for support from the sadness of the nightmare, yet there was no response.

"Please, I am so upset, and I need to talk to you, please," she begged.

"I am here, Sarah," Azra finally responded, "...but you need not call on me any longer, for I am you, and you are me. Do you understand?" Azra demanded an answer in a sharper-than-usual tone.

"Did you hurt those men, in the dream?" Sarah questioned.

"No, I did not hurt those men," she responded.

"Did I hurt those men?" Sarah questioned, now with a great deal of fear in her voice.

"No, Sarah, you did not hurt those men, either," she stated, and continued, "...but the one who did is looking for you."

"You must understand that you will only be safe if you learn to trust me and embrace our union," Azra attempted to calm Sarah down from this revelation.

"I will, and, I do. I fully embrace our union and I promise to allow you to protect me," Sarah committed her full allegiance.

"Good, Sarah, you are safe with me," reassured Azra.

"Thank you for your protection," Sarah repeated over and over again as she fell back to sleep.

Johanna

Johanna opened her eyes and looked at the small alarm clock in her room at the hostel to see it was exactly 3:00 am. Before her journey to Hong Kong, this was the only time of day that Johanna could stand to be awake, and she thought about that as she contemplated getting out of bed to take a shower while no one else was using the shared facilities. Johanna rose from the bed, showered and changed into clothing that she purchased on her way to the hostel, earlier the previous day.

She couldn't get the young woman out of her head and the name she used with the front desk attendant.

Was it just a coincidence that this was the same name the young man in Hong Kong was shouting to her as he was being struck by the bus?

Did the woman leaving the hostel know him?

Just then, Johanna was struck with a terrible feeling. "What if the woman knew what happened and was dropping a hint for her to hear?" Johanna audibly asked herself and collapsed with intense worry.

"What if she followed me here to investigate the death of the man from the alley as well as the young man from the hotel?" Johanna voiced to herself with a slight paranoia.

She sat on the twin bed, thinking of what to do about the woman she encountered when she arrived at the hostel.

Johanna retrieved the paper with the translation of the letter, as well as the woman's name and phone number, and studied what she copied from the ledger:

Sarah Martin, 410-555-3483

Johanna stared at the number, wondering what to do. If she called Sarah, what would she say to her? If Sarah wanted to know where she got her number, she would have to say that she waited for the attendant to leave the desk, to steal the number from the ledger.

Sarah would ask the reason for calling her, and Johanna would have no choice but to tell her about Hong Kong, Azra, and the young man.

If Sarah was secretly in New York to *find* Johanna,

this would certainly display her guilt.

Johanna realized she would need to approach Sarah with a certain degree of anonymity until she was sure of her intentions. She also realized that if Sarah was here to take her back to Hong Kong, she would need to appropriately *deal* with it. Johanna was prepared to eliminate any threat to her attempt at a new life. Johanna was shaking and sweating, preparing for anything.

"Am I being irrational?"

"No, of course not, what are the chances anyone would know *that* name?"

"How did she find me? I found this hostel by mistake."

"She's a spy. She's a spy and she's looking for me."

"Wait, maybe she's looking for the letter, maybe she was the one who was supposed to receive the letter."

She was clearly losing her grip with the reality of the moment and she was spiraling fast.

At 7:00 am, Johanna left her room and made her way to the front desk and asked to use the telephone. She decided she could easily pose as someone from the hostel to inform Sarah that a letter came for her after she left yesterday. She would then arrange to meet Sarah and find a way to ask her questions. She would need a disguise as well, just in case Sarah was looking for someone with her physical description.

Johanna was frantic with suspicion and had to get to the bottom of why Sarah used that name. She realized she wouldn't be able to safely remain in New York with someone following her, and she also needed to find out if this was more than just a coincidence.

Johanna picked up the phone and dialed Sarah's phone number, nervously anticipating her answering.

It rang once, twice, three times, then four…"Heh-llo?" Sarah answered the phone, clearly having been woken up.

"Yes, uhm, hi, is this Sarah?" Johanna hesitantly asked.

"Yes, well, this is Azra, but also, Sarah," she responded.

"Oh, hello Azra, my name is Jenny and I am calling from the Hell's Kitchen Hostel," continued Johanna.

"Oh hey, uhm, can I help you?" Sarah questioned. "Did my credit card get declined?" she now sounded a bit more frustrated.

"Oh, no, nothing like that, but you did receive an envelope here at the front desk after you had left," replied Johanna. "I would be happy to meet you to deliver it to you."

"Uhm, well, do you think you could mail it to me, instead…I, I just moved here, and I have a crazy schedule this week," requested Sarah.

"Of course, what's the address," replied Johanna.

Sarah gave the address to Johanna and they ended the relatively benign phone call.

Johanna noticed a pair of scissors on the front desk

near the computer and the telephone. She grabbed the scissors and took them into the lobby restroom where she began to cut her long, straight, black hair into a very short, pixie-style cut. The edges were choppy, and it was obviously not the most glamourous style, but it really "wasn't all that bad," she thought to herself.

Johanna walked out of the lobby and into the street to find Sarah, feeling a bit lighter and a bit braver.

Clayton

It was Clayton's first night in the new apartment and his head was swarming with every emotion. He was excited to begin a new chapter in the epicenter of the culinary world, and grateful for this opportunity, but he was also missing his support system from home. Clayton's mother was always a source of strength for him. He watched her overcome the mysterious loss of her husband, to raise Clayton to be the man he was today. She was selfless over the last two decades and no matter how many times she insisted he take this opportunity to move to New York, Clayton couldn't help but feel guilty for leaving her alone in Sydney.

After Jim's disappearance so many years ago, Sandy focused on one thing, her son, Clayton. She ensured he was insulated from the rumors and the speculation over the disappearance of the yacht, and she worked hard to provide her son with a life that two parents would have brought him.

"I will repay you, you'll see," Clayton whispered to himself as he studied a picture of his mother he kept in his wallet.

Clayton was exhausted from moving halfway around the world and needed to rest his mind, more than anything else. He closed his eyes and put on his headphones to drown out the noise from the street below, which he knew would be something he'd have to get used to in the "city that never sleeps." Clayton loved the sound of the cello, and his "Classical Music – Cello" playlist was exactly what he needed on this night, something familiar, soothing and reminiscent of home.

As the warm sound of the cello vibrated from his headphones into Clayton's ears, it filled him with a warm nostalgia, a sense of security, and he quickly began to lose consciousness after only a few moments. Clayton fell into a sleep so deep it would have been almost impossible for him to be awakened. Once again, his eyes were visibly jetting back and forth under his eyelids as he began to fall further into REM sleep, where he would encounter the house from his dream on the plane.

The fog dissipated in front of Clayton's eyes, and he could see the house from his previous dream. It stood there, dull and drab against the backdrop of a royal blue sky and far-off, snow-capped mountains. This time, the house wasn't the only structure in Clayton's dream, there was also a barn several hundred feet behind and to the left of the house. The barn was obviously newly renovated, with a fresh coat of dark stain coating the exterior and newly laid gravel covering the driveway from the house.

There was no little girl in the window of the house, as before, so Clayton decided to walk toward the barn, thinking that perhaps the little girl could be there. He took a deep breath and walked slowly onto the fresh gravel, worried he was making too much noise and might scare the little girl away and back into hiding. Just as he approached the door of the barn, Clayton could hear voices coming from within, and walked to the crack between the large barn door and its hinges to try to catch a glimpse of what was going on inside.

The barn was filled with rows of people dressed in suits and solid colored dresses. Men, women and children were arranged in perfectly straight rows of pews where everyone's undivided attention was focused on what looked like a church altar. Although the former interior of the barn was still very noticeable, it had obviously been converted into a church. Clayton strained to look from another angle to get a better view of the altar, where he was able to see a man, in a long grey coat, speaking to the group below that was arranged in rows like a full congregation.

As Clayton struggled to see the man and hear what he was saying to the congregation, he accidently slipped on the gravel and struck the barn door, making a very loud banging sound. Just then, the man turned his head, and everyone else turned completely around, with a snap of their heads, all at exactly the same time. Their eyes were black, deep voids and Clayton felt his heart begin to race as he backed away from the crack in the door. He slipped on the gravel again, falling to his knees as he tried to turn and run away. He got back on his feet and ran toward the house, noticing a back door under a small awning. Clayton rushed to the door and, thankfully, it was unlocked. He rushed in, slamming the door and locking it behind him.

Inside the back door where he entered, was a kitchen with only a small table and chairs inside. The room was silent and stale as if it had never actually been used as a kitchen, no remnants of food, or of eating to be seen. Clayton wanted to find somewhere to hide as he was sure that, any moment now, everyone from the barn would be breaking through the door and into the house to look for him.

Clayton opened the pantry which was completely empty, and he walked inside, closed the door, and tried to hold his breath so that no one could hear his labored, shallow breathing. A few seconds passed, a minute, then a few minutes passed, and nothing. No one came to the back door, the front door, or even a window. Clayton was confused that no one would try to find him or ask him what he was doing on the property. Slowly, he came out of the pantry and saw an open door leading to the basement of the house. Clayton stood at the top of the stairs to the basement and called, "Hello...little girl...are you down there?"

There was no response, but Clayton could have sworn the open basement door wasn't there when he first entered the kitchen. What if someone slipped into the basement while he was hiding in the pantry? What if it was the little girl and she was reaching out to him again to find her? He remembered the message she left him, "I'm waiting," which gave him the courage to make his way down the stairs and into the dark basement. Clayton reached the last step and called again for the little girl, "Hello," he said with a great deal of hesitation.

"Beep...beep...beep..." the sound of a machine, making a consistent, beeping noise was glowing green from across the musty, dark room. Clayton walked toward the green light as it continued to beep, but as he walked closer, the beeping was getting faster and faster. As the beeping continued, Clayton noticed his heartbeat was in sync with the sounds; the machine was an EKG monitor, the kind you would see in a hospital room.

He walked to the monitor and rested his hands on the side rails of an empty gurney, staring at the pattern on the machine. As he studied the green line pulsing with the sound and with his own heartbeat, he noticed something in the periphery of his vision, just below his hands on the bed. As he strained to see what was there on the gurney, visible only by the green hue from the machine was the word, "Balance," written on the white single sheet covering it.

"Balance?" Clayton whispered to himself.

The writing was peculiarly written in paint, he thought, looking at it even closer. With his face only a few inches from the word, Clayton discerned that it wasn't paint at all, but it had been written in a deep, crimson colored liquid. The smell was raw and sickening, and he knew immediately it was written in blood. As Clayton made this discovery, his heart started to race with the speed and depth of a drum. The EKG was racing with his heartbeat, faster and faster until it came to a single, sustained flat line that got louder and louder until he was jolted awake with a fist pounding on his chest in the back of an ambulance wailing through the nighttime New York City streets.

"Clayton...Clayton, can you hear me, Clayton?" shouted the paramedic that was, apparently, performing CPR on him. Clayton opened his eyes, confused and gasping for air, noticing the steady beeping of the EKG machine next to him in the ambulance.

"I can hear you, I...what happened, where am I?" Clayton asked the strangers who were all staring at him in amazement.

Clayton heard, "I couldn't wake you up. I heard you screaming in your sleep...I just wanted to make sure you weren't dead or anything," Scott hurriedly responded.

"You had what appears to be a massive heart attack in your sleep, Clayton," added the EMT who performed the CPR that brought Clayton out of his dream and into the back of the ambulance, and, apparently, back to life.

"A heart attack?" questioned Clayton, "How can I have a heart attack, I am still in my twenties?"

"Could be hereditary," responded another EMT that was checking Clayton's blood pressure.

"Do your mother or father have any history of heart disease?" she questioned him.

"I, I...don't really know," he responded, trying to understand everything that was happening, as well as still reeling from the dream.

Clayton was admitted to the Presbyterian Hospital coronary care unit, to be monitored for several days due to the severity of the heart attack that he suffered in his sleep. Clayton spent the first evening alone, thinking about the barn in his dream and the basement gurney, the blood, and the little girl.

Could this all be tied together?

Was this his body's way of telling him that something was going to happen to his heart?

Clayton wasn't sure what to think of his dreams, or his sudden heart attack. He knew he needed to call his mother to ask her some questions about his father. He wasn't sure how he was going to talk to her and, somehow, not worry her and let her know he was in the hospital. If she knew he was recovering from a massive heart attack, "She may just have one herself," Clayton thought.

CHAPTER 8 – BURGEONING FRIENDSHIP

Johanna/Sarah

J ohanna followed the map to the address that Sarah gave her over the telephone. Sarah wouldn't be expecting Johanna to simply show up at her apartment, nor was Johanna prepared to provide her with an explanation for doing so. Also, Johanna had no letter to give Sarah, since Johanna made up a fictional reason just to contact her, so she was trying to think fast while she walked.

Johanna arrived at the front of the building where Sarah was living and rang the buzzer for apartment C4. There was no immediate answer, so Johanna waited another few seconds and rang the buzzer again.

"Hello?" Sarah spoke through the intercom.

"Yeah, Hi, Azra?" Johanna answered, "It's Jenny from the hostel."

"Oh, right, hey, what's up?" Sarah hesitantly greeted Johanna with a slight tone of annoyance.

"Well, I'm embarrassed to say this, but I can't find the letter that came for you and I didn't want to just not send you anything after I called...I thought I would come and apologize for misplacing it," Johanna replied with the best excuse she could think of on the walk from the hostel to the apartment.

"Oh, well, I hope it wasn't anything important, but, it's really no problem," replied Sarah, "Hey, listen, I was about to head out for coffee before I run some errands, would you like to come?"

"Sure, I can apologize in person," Johanna quickly responded.

"Oh, don't mention it, if it was that urgent, they'll send it again," Sarah's tone a bit more relaxed, "Hold on, I'll be right down."

Johanna stiffened up and reminded herself to act normal and not like someone who just flew to New York after killing a stranger and witnessing the horrific accident of another, and it was the second stranger in less than a week's time to utter that unusual name in her presence.

The few moments that Johanna waited for Sarah to come to the door were difficult for her. Tears began to well in her eyes as she felt as though she was losing her mind. She didn't ask for these circumstances, she didn't ask to be taken from a home she didn't remember; she didn't ask to live in such a deep and dark depression that she contemplated suicide daily; she didn't ask to hear voices in her sleep directing her to fly all over the world and accidently murder a stranger. She didn't ask for "Azra" to be a new obsession in her life. Johanna knew her mind was changing and, if she didn't get a handle on things, she could easily go to a place from where she may never return.

Just then the door opened and there stood a woman considerably younger than Johanna, a woman that had a story behind her eyes and reminded Johanna of herself. She had seen that story in her own eyes, a story of grief, loneliness and confusion.

"Hey!" Johanna said immediately, before Sarah had a chance to speak.

"Hi, Jenny, thanks again for coming all this way just to tell me that you couldn't find the letter," replied Sarah, which made Johanna feel much more comfortable.

Sarah continued, "I found this small, no-frills café a few blocks from here, does that work for you?"

"It works for me, just fine!" replied Johanna with a smile on her face, wondering how she was going to get information about Azra out of a casual conversation with Sarah.

"You look so familiar to me, Jenny, have we ever met anywhere else, before today?" Sarah asked Johanna.

"I am almost one-hundred percent sure that isn't possible," Johanna responded with a slight lilt in her voice.

Sarah and Johanna sat and chatted about what brought each of them to the city. Sarah explained she had been living away from her parents' home since she was young and decided it was time for a change now that she was old enough to take care of herself.

Johanna talked about her decision to go to a place where no one else would know her, to start over and finally be at peace. Both women were surprised at how much they actually had in common, especially since there was such a large age difference between them.

"Thanks again for being so nice to me," Sarah said with complete sincerity.

"Of course, I didn't want you to get the wrong idea about my intentions," replied Johanna. "Again, I really am sorry about the letter," she continued, truly feeling sorry, even though she completely fabricated the entire story.

As Johanna walked back to the hostel, she thought a lot about her time with Sarah. She no longer worried about her secretly investigating her, in fact, she thought the two of them could become friends. Johanna paused to think about the idea of having a friend. It had been years since she remembered being that close to anyone, since her dear nurse at the hospital, the nurse with whom she shared a name.

Sarah arrived home for the evening, after starting her day with Johanna and finishing the day exploring New York. She had never felt better about life and she was finding that the city made her feel more alive than ever before. She made herself a cup of peppermint tea and sat on the floor in the living room of the apartment to simply be present.

Just as she took her first sip of tea, she was struck by the intense heat of the liquid, far hotter than she expected. The mug fell from her hand and shattered into pieces, spilling hot tea on her legs and the floor. Azra began to speak in an angry tone while Sarah tried to recover from the searing pain of the hot liquid, "Sarah, I have to talk to you about your *friend*, Jenny."

"Jenny, *my friend*?" Sarah questioned. "The woman from the hostel isn't a friend, she's just someone I met today for the first time."

"Yes, I know, but you need to be mindful of the people that are drawn to you, remember, there are others looking for you," warned Azra, "I am looking out for you, for us."

"Thank you, I will be more careful in the future," Sarah responded in a rather meek voice.

"Good, I am truly the only one you can trust right now," Azra insisted.

Over the next few days, Johanna reached out to Sarah to attempt to keep their friendship evolving, but Sarah became more and more distant. Johanna's paranoia began to creep back into her mind while she played out any and all possible scenarios that could explain Sarah's coldness, until Johanna decided that she had to take matters into her own hands and talk to Sarah. Johanna was going to confide in Sarah that she, too, knew the name Azra, and this unique coincidence was a sign that the two of them were meant to be friends.

"Yes, that'll show Sarah I can be there for her and she can be there for me, too," Johanna desperately thought to herself as she planned how she was going to persuade Sarah to develop a friendship, and not just any friendship, but a *best* friendship.

Johanna needed this friendship for her own sanity, to protect her from the days and nights that used to be so unbearable and to help her forget about the man in the alley and the young man in front of the hotel.

After a few days of not hearing from Sarah, Johanna decided to pay her an in-person visit. The inner dialogue of Johanna's desperation was getting the best of her. She needed this relationship to save her from the lonely times she used to know, and she was convinced Sarah was just as interested in knowing her.

It was Azra, Sarah's alternate identity, that wanted to keep them apart; she knew the two women were not supposed to interact with one another. The two served the same mission but neither of them was aware of this fateful detail about themselves, but soon, it would be revealed.

Johanna arrived at Sarah's building's doorstep late one evening, much later than what was traditionally expected for two people that barely knew one another. Johanna rang the doorbell and Sarah answered the intercom with hesitation, "Hello?" the surprise evident in her voice.

"Hey, it's...it's Jenny, Jenny from the hostel," Johanna mustered the courage to say when her instincts told her to turn and run from the door.

"Jenny, it's late, I really have a lot to do very early tomorrow, can I call you?" asked Sarah.

"I could really use a friend," Johanna meekly responded, hoping Sarah could relate and allow her to come inside.

"Oh, ok, well, you can come in, but only for a few minutes, I need to get some sleep tonight." Sarah attempted to provide parameters to keep this visit short and also appease Azra's cautionary warning against becoming too close to anyone.

"Thanks, I just need a friend to talk to, I won't take too much of your time," said Johanna, graciously.

The two ladies sat together, quietly, until Johanna mustered the courage to ask Sarah a question that took her by surprise, "Are you avoiding me?"

"No, of course not, why would you think that?" responded Sarah.

"Well, I have been trying to talk to you for a few days and you haven't responded to my messages," replied Johanna.

"Oh, I...I just have a lot going on with the move and I have also been looking for a job, the city's expensive, ya know?" Sarah was very good at lying on her feet, as she had done for years with her mother.

"Sure, yeah," Johanna nervously laughed, knowing this was nothing but an excuse.

Johanna knew she needed to get everything off her chest, tonight, in order to ensure that Sarah would know her story and to salvage the relationship before it was too late. Johanna just knew these details would cement their friendship.

"Listen, I have something to tell you, something that may sound a bit unbelievable, but something you may be interested in knowing," Johanna spoke while avoiding eye contact with Sarah. "I am not who you think I am. My real name is Johanna, and I am someone that also knows of the name you call yourself," she blurted it all out before she decided against it.

"The name that I call myself?" questioned Sarah.

"Yes, the name Azra is a name that has recently come into my life but is just as much of a mystery to me as the person that I heard shouting the name," Johanna said while tears began to form in her eyes.

Sarah wasn't confused by this statement at all, in fact, this was exactly what Azra brought to Sarah in her dream. As Johanna spoke, Azra began to silently provide commentary for Sarah, "This is the one that I was warning you about, this is the person who is trying to blame you for the murders that *she* committed."

Johanna continued, "A young man was shouting this name to me as he chased me. I wasn't aware of what he was saying, and it frightened me."

Johanna saw the surprise and fear in Sarah's eyes, so she started to explain herself further to try to get Sarah to see that she wasn't lying and posed no threat to her. "The man frightened me because of my past with men, the violent past that I no longer remember," Johanna pleaded with Sarah as her face became more and more twisted.

Johanna wasn't aware, though, that Azra spoke directly to Sarah during her confession and told her Johanna was a danger to her and would try to kill her as well.

Johanna continued, "I attacked a man a few days before I heard the name, Azra, in an alley in Hong Kong."

"He was approaching me in the dark and I thought he was going to hurt me. You see, I was abducted many years ago and I have developed an instinctual fear." Johanna was spinning out of control with her explanations as Sarah's face grew more and more concerned.

As Johanna told the story of her abduction, Sarah remembered why she thought she had seen her somewhere before their first meeting, several days ago. Johanna was the woman in her dreams and her visions; she was the sad woman with the gun and the woman that was always running from something. Sarah knew this woman from years of witnessing her sadness.

At the moment of this revelation, the most vivid vision that Sarah ever had flashed in front of her eyes. It was the scene of Johanna's abduction, when she was taken in the middle of the night while she slept. A small group of men put a cotton hood over her head so she wasn't able to see, and her arms and legs were bound so she couldn't walk or fight back. While the men wrestled her out of the house, in the early hours of the morning, another man stood watching, holding a thick stack of money, with tears in his eyes. This man didn't speak or move, but Sarah could tell he was close to Johanna.

Immediately, she felt an anger grow inside herself and she started to feel her consciousness shift from the compassionate Sarah to the driven and harsher Azra. The men in Sarah's vision were violent and unstoppable as they worked to keep Johanna bound and quiet, and then, all of a sudden, they used the name "Azra" while they struggled to keep her still.

"Azra, you are serving your family by allowing yourself to be sold in exchange for money that will secure a promising future for your son," one of her assailants shouted as he sat his entire body weight on Johanna's back.

Sarah was completely shocked by the use of the name in her vision.

"I think you should go," interrupted Sarah, so that she wouldn't follow through with what Azra told her to do to Johanna. "Please, go now, leave, NOW!" Sarah demanded.

"What, why?" asked Johanna, "Where did you hear this name, it is an unusual name, and it seems like such a strange coincidence that we both know this name," pleaded Johanna.

"LEAVE!" repeated Sarah as Azra demanded that

she attack Johanna before she had the chance to first harm her.

Just as Johanna got up to leave, Azra took over Sarah's body. Sarah couldn't control her arms or legs any longer and approached Johanna as she attempted to create distance between them.

"What are you doing?" Johanna spoke with fear in her voice.

"I am doing what is necessary," said Azra.

"As long as I am Azra, you are not to mention this name," she spoke again, causing Johanna to become more and more confused with Sarah's actions. Sarah no longer was present, and Azra was going to ensure she eliminated the danger she perceived from Johanna.

Azra, having fully taken over Sarah's body, pushed Johanna against the wall so forcefully that she hit her head and lost consciousness.

"What have you done?" Sarah yelled after witnessing the event.

"I am trying to help you!" Azra responded with anger, "Now, look for anything dangerous or any evidence that could show she was here," she demanded.

Sarah began to cry and started to feel fearful of Azra as she searched through Johanna's clothing. She found only a wallet, keys to her room at the hostel, and white papers that were haphazardly folded and placed in the back pocket of her jeans. Azra reassured Sarah that Johanna was here to hurt her, and that she was the one that murdered the men in Sarah's dreams. Sarah believed her, but was still very upset for the way she began to speak to her. Azra took over her physical body and that had never happened before this evening.

After Sarah looked through Johanna's wallet, she opened up the folded papers and saw it was a letter, one written in what looked like Chinese lettering and another that was written in English.

"Read the letter," demanded Azra.

Sarah agreed, to satisfy her own curiosity but also to confirm what Azra had been telling her about Johanna. Perhaps, Johanna was there to harm her, or she really was only interested in being her friend. Johanna seemed very fragile and seeing her slumped over against the wall was upsetting to Sarah.

Sarah wasn't sure why there was a letter written in a different language, but she disregarded it and took the letter written in English and reviewed the words written on the crumpled, worn paper:

> *Dear Fellow Original,*
> *I am sure that you are getting along with life much as I was before I received a letter very similar to this one. Before I go on further, I would like to tell you that I, too, lived a life of sadness and tragedy through most of my journey on Earth.*
> *You are a part of a long line of people called Originals, chosen to protect the future of hu-*

mankind. After the way humans have treated you, thus far in your life, I am sure you may need further explanation, so I will provide that to you.

I received a letter from the Original before me as well, only it had come very late in my life. This letter is much more effective when it is delivered as early in the next Original's life as possible, so that it can help to end the pain you, and others, have felt.

You begin a process called a Legacy, in which you are the first in your line of succession of other chosen humans...

As Johanna had also discovered in Hong Kong, there was a message written at the bottom of this letter that read, "Sorry, I did not get to finish the translation, I have a customer!"

Immediately, Azra began speaking to Sarah, "We need to take this letter to someone for a complete translation."

Sarah understood that the letter written in what looked like Chinese, was the original letter, and she agreed to find someone to translate it, to find out what it was referencing.

Azra coldly remarked, "This *Johanna* is too weak to be anything important and is not the recipient of this message."

Sarah responded, "How do you know, what if she is meant to protect us?"

"She lied to us about who she was for *companion-ship*; that isn't the mark of a great protector." Azra was becoming very impatient with Sarah's naivety.

Sarah sensed the shift in her tone and realized that Azra was now in control. Sarah never would have hurt Johanna, nor would she have stolen the letter from her. She was worried about what Azra was going to do to Johanna.

"Sarah, we have to get Johanna out of this apartment before she regains consciousness," she coldly instructed.

Sarah immediately responded, "Where should we take her?" fearing the response she would receive.

"We will have to put her somewhere she will not be a threat to us," Azra plainly stated. "Call the police and tell them everything Johanna admitted to you."

Sarah didn't know what to do, but she couldn't second guess Azra, especially now that she seemed to be an equal part of her and knew her thoughts and controlled her actions.

"Sarah, I know what is best for you, and I have provided you the chance to live a normal life, without the pain, without the crippling mood swings, and without the visions." Azra reminded Sarah that she needed her. "You will listen to me, as I have been listening to you for years."

Sarah agreed that Azra had helped her live a life free of the pain she used to feel during her episodes of extreme happiness and hope, to unexplained lows of gut-wrenching sadness.

"You're right, I am grateful for your protection, and you do know what is best," Sarah conceded.

"Good, now call the police, quickly, before she wakes up to fight back," Azra demanded, now realizing that her influence over Sarah had reached the level that would allow her to *be* Sarah.

Sarah slowly picked up the phone and dialed 911, as tears began to stream down her face. She realized she hadn't cried for a long time; crying used to hold little meaning to Sarah. Crying felt as it should now with Azra by her side; she was beginning to *feel* again and not simply be a prisoner to her emotions and her grief.

The police and paramedics arrived at the apartment soon after Sarah placed the call to 911. They revived Johanna and placed her under arrest for assault after Sarah explained how Johanna "became erratic and violent" and slipped and fell during her rage. Johanna couldn't remember anything about the altercation and had very little memory of anything that happened after she arrived at Sarah's apartment. She apologized to Sarah and the police, as she was being handcuffed and led out into the night.

Johanna was placed in a police car after being cleared by the paramedics and began to cry. She was confused and unclear as to what occurred that night as she recovered from her head injury. Johanna was taken to the police station to be booked, fingerprinted and interviewed about the evening at the apartment.

Once Johanna was processed, she was placed in an interrogation room at the station and was met by two detectives, Detective Smitty and Detective Albert. Smitty was an older woman, about Johanna's age, and Albert was a younger man with a kind face. Both detectives reassured Johanna that she was only being interviewed because Sarah claimed that she attempted to harm her. They needed to understand what happened before they were able to make any final determination of charges.

"To be honest, I just don't remember what happened tonight," Johanna honestly explained. "I remember confiding in Sarah about my past, and the next thing I remember, I am being revived by paramedics and surrounded by police."

Smitty looked at her partner, motioned toward the door, and told Johanna they needed to chat outside for a minute. Johanna was agreeable and was obviously distraught about what had occurred just a few hours ago.

Smitty then entered alone and asked Johanna to talk about her past, if she felt comfortable doing so. Smitty reassured Johanna that she would feel better if she talked about it, and also told her she would help her, if possible. Smitty asked Johanna if she wanted anything, like water or coffee, and Johanna asked for a glass of water, leaving her alone to think for a few minutes.

Johanna decided to talk to Smitty. Over the course

of the next few hours, she revisited what she knew of her abduction and assault, her hospital stay and identity change, the years of depression and suicidal thoughts, her dreams about a young boy and her trip to Hong Kong to find him, as well as her fateful encounter in the alley and the accident in front of the hotel.

After Johanna finished her harrowing story, Smitty sat, speechless, wondering if all this was true and what to do about this new information. Smitty knew Johanna needed help, and asked Johanna if she would consent to voluntarily admitting herself for psychological evaluation as well as a physical by a medical doctor. Johanna agreed, feeling a great weight lifted off her shoulders, and she was transported to a facility a few miles away within the network of the New York State Office of Mental Health. Smitty informed Johanna that this voluntary admission would require her to stay at the facility until it was deemed safe for her to leave by a licensed mental health professional, as well as cleared by the New York State Department of Justice. Johanna agreed and was actually relieved that she was no longer running from her past.

CHAPTER 9 – DISCOVERY

Sarah/Azra

Azra was pleased with Sarah's willingness to co-operate with her demands and could see a direct path to the mission that she was sent to accomplish. What Sarah didn't know was that Azra wasn't simply an alter ego, or a figment of her imaginative psychosis, but a being that was part of a larger plan. Azra was ready for Sarah to understand this plan so she could take over her entire consciousness.

"Now is the time to read the entire letter, Sarah," Azra asserted once everyone had vacated the apartment and she was left to be alone with her host.

"How will we do that?" questioned Sarah.

"We will seek out a translator, tomorrow, at the library, where we can inquire about the language of the letter," directed Azra.

"I am tired, please allow me to get some rest," pleaded Sarah.

"Of course, Sarah, now is the time for rest. Tomorrow will be the start of a very busy time for you and me," warned Azra.

Sarah didn't ask her to explain this warning, she

hadn't enough energy to start any new conversations, and she was starting to fear her. Sarah felt a shift in Azra, as well as herself, sensing a gradual, but present change. Sarah started to feel a loss of herself and she knew that she no longer completely owned her own thoughts.

Sarah drifted into unconsciousness as her problems from that evening melted into the background of her mind. As she fell into a deeper sleep, she noticed she was still very much aware of her surroundings. The room where she was sleeping was changing around her and she didn't understand what was happening. Slowly, the white walled room was turning darker, and the soft carpeted floor was getting harder and colder. The bed where she slept was shrinking from a plush, soft bed, to a stiff, small cot. The floor was now made of concrete, as were the dark walls, and a gate jetted from the ceiling to the floor. Sarah was no longer in the bedroom of the apartment she was renting, but now in a prison cell.

As the bedroom transformed into the cold prison cell, Sarah called for Azra, "Azra, help me, something is happening, I need you!" she cried.

Azra appeared on the other side of the steel bars. "Sarah, you have been a good host, but I have grown tired of your control," she announced with a slight smirk on her face. Sarah could see her, and she looked exactly like Sarah, just different in facial expression. Sarah was inherently kind but Azra was inherently unkind, and that was evident when looking at them, side-by-side. The physical manifestation of Azra was complete.

The next morning, Azra woke up and realized she was no longer restrained by the limits of Sarah's humanity. She would find a translator, and the letter would lead her to the person for whom the letter was intended, the Original.

Soon after arriving at the Columbus Library in Hell's Kitchen, she provided the letter to a reference librarian who told her the letter was written in Mandarin and her colleague would be able to translate it for her. She agreed to wait for the translation and made her way to the computers provided for public use, to pass the time. While waiting, she searched the internet for news relating to the men Johanna had discussed last night in her confession to Sarah.

Azra searched for law enforcement alerts in the area of the hotel Johanna had mentioned the previous evening. There were a few minor noise disturbances and a hit and run incident involving a few parked cars. Just then, there it was, an article that covered two incidents in the same neighborhood: one man struck by a city bus and another found stabbed in an alley. Azra felt fairly certain Johanna would be out of the picture now that she was taken into custody.

She was right, Johanna would not be bothering her any longer now that she was required to remain admitted to a facility within the New York State Office of Mental Health until deemed otherwise by a medical doctor and law enforcement.

Just as Azra finished re-reading the circumstances surrounding the situation with the man and the bus in Hong Kong, she was alerted by the research librarian that the translation was complete. The woman was grateful that Azra provided her with practice of her language knowledge as she "...doesn't get enough practice in translating this type of creative fiction." Azra simply laughed at this suggestion by the librarian and thanked her for offering to translate the letter. Once it was in her hands, she found a secluded section of the library to read what was written.

First, she read the part of the letter that had been partially translated by the woman working in the 88 Hotel in Hong Kong:

Dear Fellow Original,

I am sure that you are getting along with life much as I was before I received a letter very similar to this one. Before I go on further, I would like to tell you that I, too, lived a life of sadness and tragedy through most of my journey on Earth.

You are a part of a long line of people called Originals, chosen to protect the future of humankind. After the way humans have treated you, thus far in your life, I am sure you may need further explanation, so I will provide that to you.

I received a letter from the Original before

*me as well, only it had come very late in my
life. This letter is much more effective when it
is delivered as early in the next Original's life
as possible, so that it can help to end the pain
you, and others, have felt.*

*You begin a process called a Legacy, in
which you are the first in your line of succession of other chosen humans...*

Now, she continued to the rest of the letter that was just
translated by the reference librarian:

*...that each perform an important task that
will, hopefully, result in the continuation of
the human race.*

*There are several players in the Legacy: An
Original from the previous Legacy, two Balances, two Imbalances and the new Original
born on the death of the former Original.*

*If everything goes as planned, you will re-
ceive this message from a Balance. Both Balances will set off on their journey to you, but
only one will succeed and know of the Legacy, and the other will die never understanding the purpose of their life. The Balances
have suffered an early tragedy, but this creates
a strong-minded, focused, and talented person
worthy of this great responsibility. They will
become inherently attracted to your presence.*

*There are two Imbalances that, unknow-
ingly, suffer the fate of the current state of
humankind during each Legacy. As time pro-
gresses and humans evolve, the Imbalances*

have grown more and more unable to bear the weight of the species.

As things progress through the years, the Imbalances will have been so tortured that they will impede the journey of the Balance and prevent the Legacy from reaching its goal, and the human species will cease to exist. The Imbalances are specifically fated to sabotage the Legacy when humans can no longer keep balance in the Universe. If this happens, the Original of the new Legacy will die before, or on, their one-hundredth birthday never realizing their destiny and will never be relieved of their life of pain.

Once you receive this letter, you must begin your journey of self-realization and of the truth that humankind deserves its position on planet Earth.

You must believe in the preservation of the species even through all of your lived and learned tragedies. Once this has been achieved, and as you approach your one-hundredth birthday, you must also prepare a letter much like this one. You must then arrange that the letter is available to one of the new Balances after your death so they may then deliver it to the next Original, completing the entire Legacy cycle and passing it to the next succession of Legacy Members.

May you live your life longer in peace than in sadness.
Sincerely,
Your former Original

Azra sat, and mentally digested what she just read. She now fully knew her role in the Legacy, why she ended up with the letter, why she met Johanna, and why the name "Azra" was assigned to her. Sarah's mind made space for her, which must be the Universe's way of putting the plan to end the human race in motion. The Universe's cleverly designed web of relationships was no mistake.

Azra also knew Sarah was an inherently good person that would want to continue to serve the human race, but she was being chosen to represent an important and predetermined fate of the species. She had been installed in Sarah's consciousness to carry out what Sarah was incapable of doing.

After she understood everything contained in the letter and why she was introduced to it, Azra was even more determined to carry out her purpose. She knew it was up to her to find the Original, and the Balance, so the message would never be communicated. She would eliminate the Balance, destroy the letter, and kill the Original, thus ending the species as soon as possible. Now that Azra believed she had the obligation of an Imbalance, to prevent the Legacy from being fulfilled and ending the human race, the drive to complete her task was all she could think about, as though she could focus on nothing else.

Azra didn't know anyone, personally, in New York City, and wasn't sure where to start to find the Original or the Balances that were referenced in the letter. The letter stated that one of the Balances would die in their journey. Were there still two Balances? How old was the Original? Was it too late to reach them? Where on Earth would the Original be, anyway? She went back to the computer and scribbled down the name and phone number of the hospital where the accident victims were taken before leaving the library.

Azra decided she would focus on trying to find at least one of the Balances, so they could take her directly to the Original. The Balances were inherently attracted to the Original, so this seemed to be the best way to find them. Just as Azra was deep in thought, she looked up and her jaw dropped with the vision of the man that just sat down near her in the library.

The man who sat just a few feet away looked like an exact replica of what Sarah's father, Ron, looked like in pictures when he was a younger man. Azra wanted to talk to Sarah about this man, but she was afraid of what Sarah would say if she let her speak for them. She didn't want Sarah to interfere with the mission as she most likely would try to stop her. Azra, realizing the significance of the situation, understood this man was important to her journey and was too big of a coincidence to simply *be* a coincidence.

She stood up and purposefully dropped her cell phone in front of the young man, while pretending not to notice, as she walked toward the stairs to the main floor of the library. The phone fell several inches from him, and he ran after her to return it before she slipped out of sight.

"Excuse me, miss, you dropped your phone," the man said as he spoke to the back of Azra's head.

She smirked before she turned around and said, "Oh, my goodness, I have left this thing *everywhere*, thank you so much."

"Absolutely no problem, at all. I am just happy that I noticed before I never saw you again," the man replied.

"Well, I am happy too...that you caught me," she flirtatiously replied. "I'm Sarah, but I go by my nickname, Azra."

The young man picked up on the flirty vibe, "Nice to meet you, Azra, I'm Clayton."

CHAPTER 10 – ELLEN'S HEALING

Ellen

E llen had spent the last few weeks recovering from injuries she received on the day of the inaugural church service to "liberate" her from the "wickedness of her soul." After her wrists were cut and she momentarily succumbed to the massive amount of blood loss, she was quickly collected from the altar and rushed to the basement of the Donovan residence and placed on life support. The Donovans created a temporary intensive care unit in the house to serve as both Ellen's recovery room and also to be used when others from the congregation fell ill and needed more than simple holistic remedies.

As Ellen was collected from the altar, Father Donovan explained to the congregation that she would only survive if she was truly separated from her wicked predisposition. Ellen did survive, but it had nothing to do with her so-called evil predisposition. Ellen was a *survivor* and she had lived through a great deal of tragedy thus far in her short life. The death of her mother, and later, the suicide of her father, set her life's trajectory toward resilient strength and a rising above the adversity of her circumstances. Ellen was vulnerable and young, but she was also creating an immunity to emotions and influences outside of herself.

Ellen's strength returned slowly over the weeks and her wrists' wounds became only dark red scars. At first, Ellen was scared of what would come next from the Donovans, but as time passed by in her basement, makeshift hospital room, she very rarely ever saw Mother or Father. The Donovans solicited the services of Father's eldest sister, Evelyn Donovan, to care for Ellen while they focused on the newly opened church.

The New Order of Modern-Day Puritans had been their dream for as long as they could remember, and they weren't going to let Ellen keep them from their vision. Her "sacrifice" was largely a symbolic gesture that served as an example to the fledgling congregation of the power of Father and the type of devotion that was required of anyone that chose to be a member of this new denomination. It was nothing short of a full-time regimen of three services a week, daily bible study, as well as monthly gatherings of days-long festivals to serve at the pleasure of God and of Father Donovan.

Evelyn had been a nurse by trade before following Mother and Father to Colorado. Father was very close to his sister, and he knew he would need someone adept in medicine that he could trust to serve most of the medical needs of the congregation.

Days before Father planned his inaugural "sacrifice" of his adopted daughter, he approached his sister.

"Evelyn, God has prepared you for your place in our congregation through your training as a nurse."

Evelyn narrowed her eyes, understanding exactly what her brother proposed, "Roger, I understand the importance of an entirely self-contained community, and while I am hesitant to accept this responsibility, I will do so to help you serve your congregation."

"You will be rewarded for your service, Evelyn, both here on the farm as well as in Heaven," Father Donovan responded with gratitude for his sister's selflessness.

Their religion did not allow for visiting a doctor that was not a member of their church, as any medicinal practices still needed to follow the doctrine of Puritanism. Treatment must not serve to alleviate pain or provide convenience; it was meant to maintain life only. Ellen was never given pain medication for her deep cuts, nor was she pre-treated for possible infection, but only treated when infection occurred, which it had, several times during her stay in the basement.

Evelyn was not a kind or compassionate woman and she treated Ellen as a burden, rather than a patient. Ellen thanked Evelyn for caring for her, the first day after she regained full consciousness in the basement.

"Child, I would rather be anywhere else but here with you. It is because of your wicked ways, and it is you who needed your demons to be removed in the first place!" Evelyn snapped back at the child as she struggled to speak to Evelyn at all.

Ellen gathered the strength to respond, "I apologize for my wickedness."

Evelyn didn't accept her apology. "Wicked child, all children need to apologize for the care they receive from an adult. You are selfishly taking time away from my service to God, and God can see that," she bitingly replied.

There was original sin in just *being* a child in the Puritan religion, and not knowing things about the way of the world was a child's burden to bear. Ellen was required to pray daily to ask for forgiveness of the sin of robbing Evelyn of her time to care for Ellen's wounds and sustenance.

Evelyn was not only a source of guilt for Ellen, but also a source of physical pain. Evelyn kept Ellen secured to the hospital bed with zip ties around her ankles and around her small, thin biceps that were connected to the siderails of the gurney. Ellen was often secured in her bed for days on end, with only a few short hours of relief during her changing of clothes and the occasional bath.

Evelyn would stingingly slap Ellen on the face and body when she was frustrated that she couldn't attend a festival or a church service.

"Child, these punishments were meant to be much harsher, but I am a compassionate caretaker, I give you only as much pain as God wants you to experience," Evelyn told Ellen moments after her first experience with Evelyn's physical abuse.

Ellen never responded to Evelyn as she was being beaten in her hospital gurney. She simply stared blankly at the wall while she received each loud slap, stinging her skin more and more until the final blow that often left a red bruise similar to a brush burn on her fair, sensitive skin.

There were days, though, that Ellen wouldn't see Evelyn, which meant that she wouldn't eat or drink that day. This was bittersweet for Ellen as she wouldn't endure the painful slaps, but she would sit in the pitch-black darkness of the basement while hunger pangs coursed through her frail and neglected body. She would often hear people congregating in the kitchen, sounding as though they were enjoying themselves on the farm, and she would hear the sounds of festivals and laughing children.

Ellen wondered why she wasn't allowed to join these children and how she was different from them. After all, she was only a newborn when her mother died, and just a small child when her father took his own life. How was she to know the fate of her parents? Ellen felt guilty for the deaths of her parents, but she didn't understand how she became wicked or why she was predetermined to be wicked, as was explained to her while Evelyn slapped her.

Ellen had been told many things about herself since she was adopted by Mother and Father, some things she learned to believe and others she learned to ignore.

The Donovans weren't aware of what Ellen was and how she was impenetrable by their accusations and false beliefs of her original sin. Ellen was soon turning eleven and, at this important age, she was beginning to show early signs of becoming a woman. These early stages of the transition from childhood to adolescence also brought Ellen a great deal of clarity, even in the midst of the Donovans' conditioning.

Ellen was the Original of her Legacy, trapped in a small farmhouse in rural Colorado and locked away by her religious fundamentalist adoptive parents. The letter that was written by Li Jie, given to Li Qiang, discovered by Johanna and stolen by Azra was meant for Ellen to receive, read and act upon. The letter needed to be delivered to Ellen by a Balance before she was too old and too jaded to fulfill her destiny.

Azra had the letter and needed to reach Ellen to kill her before the Balance was aware of her identity and her mission. Now that Ellen was in the very early stages of transitioning to adulthood, her Balance was going to be able to feel her presence soon and their destiny would help draw them together. Azra was aware of this after reading the letter she was never meant to see and decided that finding the Balance, that would eventually take her to the Original, would be the only way for her to end the Legacy.

Ellen also began seeing glimpses of her purpose in her dreams. Most days, while she laid in her basement recovering, she would sleep. It was quite dark in the basement when Evelyn hadn't come to tend to her, and the only light was from the small window near the metal basement access doors on the opposite side of the room.

Ellen regularly saw a young man in her dreams who was always looking around the property, and she would view him from her bedroom window upstairs. The man was often trying to get her attention, but she was afraid to shout and anger Mother or Father; she feared them even in her dreams. Recently, she dreamt that he was in the basement with her, but she couldn't see him, only hear him. This dream ended with a sense of almost feeling him still with her in the basement, looking over her while she slept in her hospital bed. Ellen felt a connection to this young man, similar to the feeling that she shared with her father. In many ways, Ellen saw this stranger as the part of her father that disappeared long before he died, the part that was supposed to protect her and make her feel safe and secure.

After these dreams, Ellen would wake and feel as though she could deal with anything that would come her way that day. It was a way that Mother and Father, and Evelyn, could never make her feel, as they were the source of the pain in her life. The Donovans believed they were not supposed to coddle or care for Ellen but force her to develop a foundation of self-reliance that would prepare her for the rigor of life. A life that was in complete servitude of God and of Father Donovan and, eventually, a husband. Of course, Mother and Father re-peatedly told Ellen, almost immediately after taking her in as a foster child, that she was marked and wicked and would have a very difficult time ever finding a husband and ever having children of her own. Ellen was confused with these ideas, being only a child herself, but as she grew older, she would come to understand the meaning behind those words.

Now that Ellen's wounds had healed and her body had regained enough strength, she was able to leave the basement and go back to her bedroom, back to the closet where she slept. She was also able to start her chores, once again, and helped maintain the church and the de-mands of the weekly calendar.

Mother directed Evelyn to read to Ellen to ensure that she was keeping up with her scriptures and reeduca-tion while in recovery from her injuries. Before and after her recovery, Ellen was required to read the scriptures alone and recite them each day after breakfast, to prove to Mother that she was trying her very best to share in the devotion of the religion. If Ellen was not exact with her recitations, she was punished by withholding her dinner that day, which resulted in Ellen only eating one meal a day, most days of the week.

Father also told her to expect more "blood-let-ting" ceremonies any time he felt it necessary for Ellen. She feared this happening again as it was one of the most terrifying experiences of her life. Feeling the life drain almost completely out of her body as she witnessed the faces of the congregation turning white with disgust, and with utter surprise, was a vision that Ellen would see for the rest of her life. She still didn't understand why no one tried to help her, why no one thought it was unusual to almost kill a child in front of a large room of children and adults. Mother and Father told her it was her own fault they *had* to do that to her, for her own salvation, and she believed it more and more each day. Ellen felt alone in the world and she longed for her parents, sometimes even wishing for death so that she could be with them.

CHAPTER 11 – PAST
TIES REVEALED

Azra and Clayton started to become friends after their meeting at the library. Clayton felt a kinship and a bond with her that he wasn't able to explain, as if he already knew her face and her voice, which would be impossible. She was American and he just relocated from Australia and had no American ties prior to his move.

Clayton had been struggling with getting enough sleep lately, and Azra had become a welcome distraction for him. Clayton was regularly taken to the remote farm in his dreams and would occasionally catch a glimpse of a little girl observing him as he tried to reach her. He believed she left him the message, "I'm waiting," because she was calling out for help. Her repeated visits in his dreams was a sign that she could be real and could be in *real* danger.

Clayton started to trust Azra, and she could tell they were growing closer and closer as the days of their friendship passed. At first, they were strangely attracted to one another, physically, but that waned after only a few days. Their connection seemed different than romantic, different than a superficial and fleeting relationship, as if they had ties that were totally unrelated to their current life situations.

Clayton decided to confide in Azra about his dreams, the farm and the little girl. He told her about the surroundings of the farmhouse, the barn and the church, the hospital bed in the basement as well as the almost daily visits in his dreams. She knew exactly what this meant for Clayton, as well as herself, and saw these confessions as proof that Clayton was a Balance as referenced in the letter that was taken from Johanna.

Azra also decided she should proceed with caution just in case this was all too easy. How could the Balance have been so obvious to her? She assumed that finding the Balance would have taken her a very long time, after all, what were the chances that the one person she was looking for would just fall into her lap? Just as she was thinking about how coincidental this all seemed, she remembered the letter informing the Original that Legacy members were drawn to one another *because* of their affiliation. The letter was predestined to be delivered to the Original, and if Azra was going to do her part as an Imbalance, she would need to manipulate Clayton into trusting her and allowing her to follow him to the Original.

Azra met Clayton for coffee at the small coffeehouse near her sublet after he contacted her late one evening. He was unable to sleep, haunted by the dream of the little girl, and needed something to take his mind off of his thoughts. He wasn't sure why he was having these dreams and wasn't sure if these dreams meant anything important.

"What if someone is really trying to communicate with me, what if someone really is in danger?" he asked Azra, adding, "I know this sounds ridiculous that someone is trying to talk to me in my dreams, but she comes to me every night and it feels so real. I feel so helpless, like I need to help her, but I just can't find her," he said crying and obviously very upset by the dreams he was having. "What if I'm too late, what if she died in that hospital bed, what if that is why I can't find her?" he said as the tears dripped from his wet eyelashes.

"Listen, do you think that you would be drawn to her and continue to dream about her, if she was dead?" Azra questioned Clayton, truly wishing to make him feel better, but also to keep him motivated to continue to look for her. "There is nothing wrong with keeping an open mind, and at least for now, you have a connection to her and looking for her in your dreams doesn't have to impact your life when you are awake," she reassured Clayton.

"Yeah, you're right, I guess I should try to get more sleep so I can keep a level-head," Clayton remarked, embarrassed by his confessions.

"Listen, you have nothing to hide from me, I know you are a rational person and I believe there are things we can't explain about this world and about our connections to other people." Azra believed what she was telling Clayton, but also needed him to remain open to talking to her about things he would normally keep to himself. "You can trust me, Clayton," she reassured him.

"I know, and you can also trust me," Clayton responded.

"I do, I definitely do," Azra said with a blank face, knowing she was sealing his fate, and the entire race of humanity, with this lie. She was surprised at how easy it was to lie to someone about something so important, because she knew that she was doing what was expected of her. Azra was an extension of Sarah, and Sarah never would have been able to complete such an important mission; Sarah was too good, too honest, and too weak to be *this* kind of Imbalance. Azra became the dominant personality because she was doing what Sarah never could do.

Azra and Clayton talked all night at the twenty-four-hour coffee shop that was just a few blocks from her sublet apartment. Before either of them noticed, the sun was illuminating the autumn city streets with a vibrant, morning orange glow.

"Wow, it's almost quarter after seven!" Clayton remarked with surprise as he rubbed his eyes and stretched his arms, "I should probably let you get some rest."

"I like staying up late," she reassured him as she tried to hide her complete exhaustion.

Just as she was about to return her coffee mug

to the front counter, her cell phone began to ring. Her mother was calling, and it was the last person she ever expected to hear from, especially after all this time.

Clayton noticed the look on her face. "What's wrong, you look like you've seen a ghost?" he asked.

"Oh, nothing, I...I just need to answer this, excuse me for a second," she responded and walked outside to answer the call.

"Hello?" she answered the phone with a noticeably confused affectation.

"Hi Sarah, I need to talk to you, do you have a minute?" Sarah's mother responded.

"Uh, yeah, I...I do, but I may have to call you back," Azra responded, trying to make her voice as sweet and gentle as Sarah's.

"Well, I need you to come home as soon as possible, it's your father, he has passed away, Sarah," her mother revealed and began to cry. She fought through the emotion and continued her speech, "Your father's been in a terrible accident, he was fishing in the harbor, with a friend, and they were struck by an out of control speed boat," her mother rushed to get it all out before she broke down again. "The Coast Guard believed the speed boat was having mechanical issues and the operator was unable to slow it down, under no fault of their own," she just finished her sentence before completely falling to pieces. "I need you to come home to attend the funeral and to see your family, it's been so long, and I miss you."

She was completely taken off guard by this comment. Sarah's mother had never said anything remotely *motherly* to her, in her entire life.

"Of course, I will come home, when is the funeral?" Azra asked.

"The day after tomorrow," her mother responded.

"Can I bring a friend?" she asked. "He's been dealing with a lot lately and I think getting out of the city may do him, and me, some good." Azra wanted Clayton to stay close to her now that she was certain he was a Balance.

Sarah's mother agreed and the two ended the conversation. Clayton was making his way out of the coffee shop to check on Azra just as she was putting the phone in her pocket.

"Everything okay?" Clayton inquired.

"Yeah, uh, I guess so," she responded with hesitation. "It was my mother, she said my father was in an accident, and now, he's dead."

"Your father's dead?" Clayton questioned, noticing that she didn't really look too upset or bothered by this seemingly devastating news.

"He died in a boating accident," she replied without looking at him.

"A boating accident?" Clayton questioned. "That's how my dad died as well," he confided in her in hopes of making her feel like she wasn't alone.

"Really?" she asked, now looking directly into his eyes. "Would you come with me to the funeral?" she asked with as much sincerity as she could muster. "It would really help me."

"You can count me in, I just need to grab a few things from my apartment and tell my roommate that I won't be home for a few days," Clayton responded to Azra, truly wanting to be there for her during this time.

The pair headed to Clayton's apartment, greeted Scott, and gathered a few things for the trip. Azra looked at a picture Clayton had in his room of his father and what looked like Clayton as a very small child. The resemblance of Clayton's father to Clayton, and to Sarah's father, was uncanny. They looked like they were very closely related. Azra was concerned that Sarah's mother would be alarmed at this resemblance, but then she remembered this was the exact thing that attracted her to him. This similarity could be the Legacy in action, bringing them all together to find the Original. She knew that meeting Clayton was kismet, so she decided to simply let the pieces fall where they may while she maintained a strong focus on the message of the letter. Clayton and Azra both said goodbye to Scott and proceeded to her sublet before the Port Authority Bus Terminal where they would be leaving in a few hours for Baltimore.

Ron and Susan Martin moved to the United States well over two decades ago, before the birth of their daughter, Sarah. The couple was an unexpected union borne out of circumstances beyond their control. They fell in love because of this shared situation and had since grown impatient with the domestic life they built over their extended time in Baltimore. Ron and Susan were both involved in an accident, many years ago, pushing the two into isolation due to the high-profile nature of their situation. The couple spent a few months in New York City to collect money and property supplied by Susan's parents, but soon selected a less populated neighborhood in suburban Baltimore, Maryland to regroup and plan their future. Sarah was born only a year after their arrival in the US and thwarted the couple's original plans to continue moving through North America to quietly settle in a remote part of the mountain town of Whistler, British Columbia.

Sarah's mother, Susan, parked her car at the Baltimore Downtown Bus Station and decided to try to relax during the hour wait for Sarah and Clayton's bus to arrive. It was almost ten o'clock at night and she was exhausted from the last few days of planning Ron's wake and funeral. Their group of close friends and family was quite small, but Susan's grief was overwhelming. Ron was more than just a husband to Susan; he was a partner through their harrowing early experiences that brought them together as a couple. Ron was the voice of reason and source of strength for Susan when she needed it most. Susan sat in her car, seat reclined while listening to the rain dance across the roof and windshield, thinking about Ron's handsome face and gentle voice. Susan could see a group of people walking through the parking lot and recognized the silhouette of her daughter due to her familiar gait.

Susan stepped out of her car to make room for her daughter, when she caught a glimpse of Sarah's traveling companion. She couldn't believe what she was seeing. She stood in astonishment, trying to focus her eyes on the crowd exiting the bus and moving through the parking lot. She slowly walked toward the couple as they weaved through the maze of cars in front of her. Once the couple stood just a few feet from Susan, she stood there motionless and without a sound. The three of them silently gathered between two SUV's, awkwardly wondering what the other was thinking before Susan blurted out, "How the fuck did you find us?"

"Excuse me?" Clayton wanted to make sure that what he heard was truly what Azra's mother said to him before answering her strange, and a bit forward, question.

"I'm...I'm sorry, you just look a lot like someone I know," Susan apologized, realizing that Clayton had no idea who he looked like.

Azra stared blankly at Susan, trying to quickly understand what was going through Sarah's mother's head, while simultaneously realizing that she also needed to pretend to be Sarah during her stay with Susan. She wasn't too worried about pretending to be Sarah, as Susan never really knew her daughter as an adult and could pull off really any personality as "Sarah."

"Mom, I would like you to meet Clayton," She said to Susan with a look of intrigue on her face.

Susan cleared her throat, wiped a tear from the side of her face, and was barely able to utter, "Nice to meet you, Clayton. I apologize for my behavior; it's been a really hard couple of days."

"No worries, Mrs. Martin. I lost my father many years ago and I understand the unpredictability of emotions during a loss like this." Clayton used his most polite voice in his condolences, hoping that it would help to diffuse Susan's grief, even for just a moment.

"I know, Clayton," Susan stated as she looked blankly into Clayton's eyes, the eyes that looked so much like the eyes she had grown to know and love over the decades.

"You know?" Clayton questioned.

"I mean, I am sure that I now know how you must feel," Susan responded while wondering how she was going to tell the man standing before her that her dead husband was actually his long-lost father from twenty-five years ago.

Susan spent the drive from the bus terminal to the family home in complete silence as Azra and Clayton made small talk to override the awkward vibe. Azra could tell what Susan was thinking, for the most part, and was waiting to see how Clayton would respond once he arrived at the house and saw his own face looking back at him from the family photos hanging on the walls. Azra watched the confusion evolve into fear on Susan's face as she mulled over what she was going to say to Clayton.

"Clayton, how much do you know about your father?" Susan broke her strained silence, realizing he was going to discover the truth in less than eight minutes, anyway.

"Well, not too much, other than what my mother has told me," he responded. "I was only four years old when he disappeared," Clayton added.

"Do you know anything about the circumstances surrounding his disappearance?" Susan inquired.

Clayton, noticeably struggling with this question and not really sure how to answer her, simply stated, "Nothing more than what I have been hearing for the last twenty-five years of my life, that he just disappeared."

Just then, Azra noticed how uncomfortable this line of questioning was for Clayton and decided to put a stop to it before another word came out of Susan's mouth. "Mom, what is this, a cross-examination or something?"

"Shut up, Sarah, just shut up!" Susan started to cry and slammed on the brakes of the car, forcing everyone inside to violently heave forward and then backward in their seats.

"Jesus Christ, mom, are you trying to kill us?" Azra screamed.

Susan pulled the car over onto the shoulder of the two-lane, suburban road they were traveling and released her seatbelt. She turned around in her seat so she could face Clayton.

"Clayton, I don't know how to tell you this, without just coming out and saying it, but there is something that you need to know before we arrive to the house and before you meet anyone at Ron's funeral, tomorrow." Susan was now trying to get her words out over the beating of her heart.

Susan knew this day would eventually come, but after all this time, she had stopped worrying about it. Never, in her wildest dreams, did she expect her daughter to simply bring home her own half-brother, completely by chance. Susan didn't care if her daughter was sabotaging her, she was actually starting to feel relief from the guilt that she had been carrying all these years, guilt for taking a father away from his son, guilt for lying to so many people, and guilt for lying to her daughter.

"Sarah, why didn't you tell me that you met Clayton," Susan asked Azra, to try to clear up any question that she knew who he was before this moment.

"Mom, I don't...I don't understa..." Azra barely got out before Susan interrupted her.

"It doesn't matter, Sarah." She felt reasonably certain this was not her daughter's doing, but the coincidence of it all was too much to consider right now, and it was also not important.

"Clayton, my *real* name is Sonia, and Ron's real name was Jim," she continued with a fast breath and before she lost her nerve, "My dead husband, who, as you know, died only a few days ago, was your father, who disappeared twenty-five years ago with me, on my yacht."

Susan continued to tell the story to both Azra and Clayton. Azra was completely stunned by this news as it was far more extensive than she ever expected, but she was also seeing a vulnerable side to Sarah's mother that she never knew existed. Susan talked about the accident and all her former friends, and fiancé at the time, perishing at sea. Only Jim and Sonia made it out alive and her famous, wealthy, family went to great lengths to keep this a secret due to the potential devastating financial repercussions that would come from the accident.

The accident was technically the family's fault as Sonia ignored weather reports making their voyage a violation of the Australian Coast Guard. The yacht was caught in a storm one-hundred and eighty-five kilometers off the coast where it sank, dragging with it the sleeping passengers to the bottom of the sea. All passengers, and the yacht, were never found again...all but Jim and Sonia.

The couple was hidden from the public and taken to New York City. The Faberges had ties to powerful people in Australia, and in America, and used those ties to keep everything quiet, the family out of litigation and, potentially, out of criminal investigation for the deaths. The Faberges offered Jim a multi-million-dollar settlement to stay away from his family in Australia, and soon, he and Sonia fell in love and became pregnant with Sarah. The pair was kept together, confined with one another, forging the unlikely union.

Over the years, Jim expressed interest in contacting Clayton, but Sonia put a stop to it, claiming they could both be held accountable for the accident and end up in prison, now that so much time had passed and neither of them had ever gone to the authorities. Jim had also signed an agreement with the Faberge family that he would never attempt to contact Clayton or Sandy after accepting the settlement. The Faberges told Jim that they would be forced to cut him out of the family, take Sonia away from him, and freeze all of his assets if he tried to go back to his former life. Jim agreed to the arrangement with Sonia's family, knowing that he really had little choice in the matter and he slowly became desensitized to the loss of Sandy and Clayton in exchange for a new wife, child and multi-million-dollar bank account.

Initially, Clayton sat and stared at Susan with no expression on his face. He had a million different emotions running through his head, but he wasn't sure how to articulate them. He just met Susan, and Azra, and he wasn't really sure who to trust right now. He thought of asking to be taken back to the bus station to run from these feelings of surprise, betrayal, and anger, but he then realized these people could answer so many questions about the man he thought was dead for the last twenty-five years. He could see the regret in Susan's eyes, and he knew Azra hadn't known about the situation, so he decided to suspend judgment and get to know them better.

The Martins were an extension of Clayton's family, and even if he ended up hating them, he knew running away would leave him with even more questions. He was also thinking of his mother; what would she say about all of this, and should he tell her? Clayton knew that his mother, Sandy, would be absolutely devastated and would certainly make this revelation public. He wasn't sure what to do, what to believe or how to react to any of this. He swallowed the lump in his throat, looked at Azra, then at Susan, and said, "So I guess that makes you my step-mother?"

Susan, looking relieved by Clayton's response, whispered in response with tears in her eyes, "Yes, I suppose that it does."

"And, like it or not, you're my half-sister, Azra," Clayton said with a smile.

"Azra, who's Azra?" Susan questioned.

"No one, mom," she snapped back at Susan and rolled her eyes at Clayton.

Susan sat forward in her seat and took the car out of park to continue on their way home from the bus terminal. Clayton and Azra sat in the back seat, silently, and she offered her hand to Clayton. He took it, and held it softly, as he gazed out the window feeling both grateful for the chance to finally know the truth, and also trying to suppress the deep feelings of betrayal.

The rest of the car ride was silent, and all three passengers had drastically different emotions swirling through their heads. Azra was determined to keep finding clues to lead Clayton to the Original; Susan was relieved that she was able to voice the events of so many years ago; and Clayton was feeling regretful for never knowing his father, although today, he felt he knew him better than ever before.

CHAPTER 12 – FAWAD'S REVELATION

Ameer

Johanna left a wake of confusion in the neighborhood of the 88 Hotel, in Hong Kong. There were two major incidents, discovered on the same day, that were a shock to the residents and business owners in the area.

The driver of the bus that struck Ameer was inconsolable. She was a mother of three children and a model driver for the city, now on administrative leave pending an investigation by police. She lived a life of duty and service to her employer as well as her family.

The detectives looking into the murder of Li Qiang were making their rounds through the neighborhood asking for witnesses and other clues that could help bring justice for the man that was discovered dead and alone in an alley. The old couple that found the body was struggling with their discovery, made worse by the hours of questioning at the police station.

Luckily, and surprisingly, Ameer wasn't killed in the bus accident. He was placed in a medically induced coma to accommodate his recovery and aid in his healing, and until his lungs were strong enough to breathe

on their own. Ameer's father, Fawad, alerted to his condition by a phone call from a stranger, made his way to
Hong Kong to be with his son during his days in the Intensive Care Unit. Initially, Fawad was unaware that Ameer
had received information about his mother and didn't
know he had traveled to Hong Kong to find her. Fawad
assumed his wife, Azra, was long dead, as was the fate of
many trafficked women.

After arriving to the hospital where Ameer was in
the Intensive Care Unit, Fawad looked at his unconscious
son and immediately began to cry at the sight of him
looking so different from the healthy, vibrant man he had
grown to know. Fawad sat next to his son and prayed
for him, aloud, in hopes that Ameer would hear him and
know that he wasn't alone. Fawad was weighed down by
guilt, but he needed to do what was necessary, in the end.
The stranger that called Fawad convinced him to do the
unforgivable and he was struggling after seeing the state
of his only son.

The doctor eventually came to discuss with Fawad
the plan to revive Ameer now that he had spent some
time in the hospital and his lungs were ready to be removed from the respirator.

Several hours had passed since the doctor began
slowly withdrawing the drugs that kept Ameer asleep
during his intensive recovery. Slowly Ameer began to re-

gain consciousness and saw his father sleeping on a small cot provided by the hospital for family members staying with their loved ones. Ameer couldn't remember much of what had happened to him leading up to the accident, nor did he know where he was in the world.

"Well, hello, Ameer, how are you feeling?" Ameer's nurse, Shum, said to him in English, as he watched Ameer open his eyes and attempt to adjust to the light of the hospital room.

Ameer looked at Shum, asked him where he was, to which Shum responded, "You are at the Tung Wah Hospital in Hong Kong, Ameer." He continued, "You were involved in a very serious accident several weeks ago and you have just been revived from your medically-induced coma."

Ameer tried to think about what the nurse just said to him while looking at his father sleeping just a few feet from his hospital bed. "Hong Kong?" Ameer repeated to the nurse.

"Yes, Ameer, apparently you were running after someone, a woman, trying to get her attention, and you were struck by a bus as you ran into the street to follow her," Shum explained. "The police would like a few words with you when you are strong enough to talk to them."

"Thank you," Ameer responded, still looking at his father, knowing there was tension between them, but couldn't quite place why.

He was also trying to piece together the accident and remember who he was chasing after into the street. As Ameer was struggling to remember what brought him to Hong Kong, his father opened his eyes, turned to Ameer and seeing his son was awake, he started toward the hospital bed. As Fawad walked toward Ameer, everything started to rush back into his mind. Ameer remembered the letter, the discussion that he had with his father before leaving Pakistan, the airport, the hotel, and finally, the bus and the smell of the accident.

The look of panic had become quite obvious on Ameer's face and Fawad stopped at his bedside and asked, "Ameer, you are awake, what is wrong, my dear boy?"

"I found her, after all of this time and all of your lies, I found her!" Ameer responded.

"Found whom?" Fawad asked his son, attempting to become more lucid after sleeping in the cot.

"I found mom, I found Azra!" Ameer shouted at his father with no regard for the expectation to always display respect for his father in public.

"You sold her to traffickers, you betrayed her, and you betrayed me!" Ameer continued to shout at his father despite the tears streaming from his eyes, from a combination of sadness and a body not fully healed from its injuries.

"Ameer, you do not know what you are talking about, now lower your voice and help me understand why you are saying these things about your mother!"

Fawad said to Ameer, sounding more hurt than angry or defensive.

"I was given an anonymous letter, and it said that you and your brothers sold her to a gang," Ameer accused his father of exactly what was written in the letter.

"How *dare* you accuse me of something so unforgivable, Ameer!" his father responded. "I may be hard on you, and I may have my ideas about a woman's place in the family, but I provide for my family and I don't need blood-money from thugs!"

Ameer saw in his father's eyes the same grief and panic he saw the day his mother disappeared. He wasn't sure what to say to his father; his father wasn't acting like a guilty or lying man.

"Azra was an important part of the family, Ameer, she was worth more money than any *gang* could have provided," Fawad said to his son as he turned and left the room.

Ameer sat in his bed, with so many questions left to be answered. Was his mother alive after all, and was that really her in the pictures? Who sent him the letter in the first place, and why would they want him to believe his mother was alive, and betrayed, by his father?

Ameer's head was throbbing, his ribs were tender, both of his legs were broken, and he realized that now was not the time to start a feud with his father. Ameer needed to decide if he was going to believe his father before Fawad came back to the room, if he was going to come back to the room at all. Ameer realized that what he accused his father of was one of the worst things that anyone could be accused of, especially if he was wrong.

Ameer fell asleep after waiting for his father to return for over an hour. He was given another course of antibiotics and a fresh morphine drip as his pain became too intolerable to bear without it. As Ameer lay in his hospital bed, fully unconscious, the door to his room creeped open slowly and quietly. A shadowy figure made its way into the room and stood over Ameer while he slept and pulled two small syringes from their pocket. The contents of the syringes were injected into Ameer's IV bag hanging just a few feet from his body. Just as the figure entered, it slipped out of the room, without notice.

CHAPTER 13 – CLAYTON'S POSITION

Clayton

Clayton wasn't ready for Ron's viewing and funeral, but he knew that seeing his father, even in a casket, would help him move on from the tragic start he had been living with for most of his life. Susan asked Clayton to try to disguise his unmistakable resemblance to Ron so that it wouldn't raise any suspicions with their "family" in Baltimore. Susan offered him a shoulder-length, brown wig and reading glasses. Clayton looked in the mirror as he was getting in disguise and started laughing at the man looking back at him. The laughter quickly turned into tears, though, as the gravity of the situation hit him. He felt both extreme sadness as well as a great relief he had answers to questions that had haunted him for so many years.

Azra knocked on the bathroom door, letting Clayton know they were leaving in a few minutes. He pulled the wig into a short ponytail and accompanied the Martins to the funeral home where there was a small crowd gathering in the parking lot. The group of people were crying and talking of Ron, remembering his life, while

Azra and Clayton stood, in silence, taking in the attention Susan was receiving from the group. Azra was occasionally greeted by some of them, with tears in their eyes, calling her Sarah and looking sincere in their grief. It was obvious that Ron was loved by his closest friends, and that was comforting to Clayton. He knew if he was going to make it through this day, he needed to try to put his own bias and anger against his father and Susan away somewhere, for another day. Perhaps this could even help him see his father's perspective and truly understand why his father abandoned the family he left in Australia over twenty-five years ago.

At the wake, Clayton decided to sit in the back of the room, by himself, while the funeral director spoke and friends gave speeches remembering their friend, Ron. Clayton heard people speak of a man that he didn't know. He never had the chance to take vacations to the Grand Canyon, or sing karaoke at weddings with him, or any of the other things people were fondly remembering on this day. The only thing he could remember about his father was the grief associated with his mysterious disappearance, a mystery that had now been solved. "So, now what's left?" Clayton whispered to himself as he stared blankly at the open coffin several hundred feet from the chair where he was sitting.

He saw a far-away profile of his father, just barely visible from inside the silk-lined casket, which wasn't made any clearer by the reading glasses used to help disguise his father-and-son likeness. Clayton glanced toward Azra, who was sitting with her mother and greeting her father's mourners, but instead of a look of grief on her face, she looked incredibly annoyed. Clayton understood that everyone processed grief differently and tried to give her the benefit of the doubt. After all, Azra was dealing with a new reality in regard to who her parents, Ron and Susan Martin, really were. Clayton needed to make sure Azra was supported so they could rely on one another through this shared experience.

As the viewing was winding down and people were beginning to make their way to the parking lot for the funeral procession, Clayton slowly approached the casket where his father's body lie. He felt a great deal of anxiety building as he inched closer and closer to the casket. This man was a mystery to Clayton for so long and was elevated to somewhat of a God, but now, here he was, in a coffin.

His body was much smaller than he expected, much more *human* than he ever pictured his father when trying to remember what he used to look like through the years. Clayton took a deep breath and a final step toward his father and looked at him while standing directly over the casket. He began to cry while studying the face he had missed for most of his life, as the anger and contempt just melted away. The tears were mostly those of sadness and relief, knowing that the man he had wondered about for so long had lived a life filled with family and close friends, even if it wasn't Clayton's family.

The funeral was small and somber, and no one suspected that Sarah's guest was anything other than a close friend. As the coffin was lowered into the grave, Clayton decided to stand at the back of the group, which was a smart decision as the situation became too emotional for him, once again, to hide his tears. This day proved to be one of the most unexpected, but also one of the most pivotal, days of Clayton's life. He was finally able to receive the closure he had been searching for all these years.

After the wake and funeral, mostly everyone in attendance came back to the Martin house where Susan prepared a backyard feast in the tradition of the annual barbeque they were so famous for amongst their circle of friends. Ron was discussed fondly, laughs were shared, often mixed with short bursts of tears, and eventually the group thinned as everyone started to make their way home from the long day of Ron's memorial.

Clayton became very tired and asked Susan if he could lie down. Susan, of course, understood that Clayton had a very difficult day and decided to postpone her conversation regarding next steps for settling the estate with him. Ron's will was very specific in stating that in the event that he died before his wife, she would promise to anonymously leave Clayton half of his assets, and she would then keep the other half. Susan had her doubts about this but agreed to the arrangement to concede to

Ron on his last attempt to contact his son and former wife. Now that Clayton and Susan had met, she realized there was no danger in fulfilling the request, and she had no plan to report it to her family, at least, in the immediate future. As Clayton made his way to the downstairs spare bedroom, Susan excused herself to make a phone call.

Susan stepped into the dining room and retrieved her cell phone from her pocket. "Hi, Mary, this is Susan, I have some tragic news about Ron," she greeted the woman on the other end of the phone call.

"Ron was killed in a boating accident last week, Mary. Sarah is here and we just got home from the funeral," Susan continued. "I realize that Ron was supposed to arrive on the farm in a few days, but we have been so blindsided by everything that I completely forgot to call you before now."

"Oh, Susan, God Bless you for your call and your concern at such a difficult time," Mary responded to Susan. "The Donovan family and church should be your very last concern right now and know we are here to help you and your family with anything that we may be able to offer," she continued.

"Thank you, Mary, will you be able to appoint someone else to Ron's position before your holiday celebrations begin?" Susan inquired.

Mary replied, "Well, Ron was very special and very talented, so it won't be an easy task."

Roger Donovan was visiting the east coast several weeks ago to purchase medical supplies from a friend in pharmaceutical sales that had a connection to restock their basement hospital. The care that was provided to Ellen during her recovery depleted most of their medical resources and it was essential to keep their private care needs available to the congregation. Ron and Roger met at a restaurant liquidation sale on the day Roger was planning to drive back to Colorado. The men met during a bidding war for a very diverse collection of flatware which began their introductions to one another. Ron told Roger about his former career as a chef for the very wealthy and Roger explained his desperate need for a private chef for the weeks between the Thanksgiving and Christmas holidays.

Roger explained that his church did not celebrate Christmas in the traditional sense, but it was regarded as a season of gratitude for the abundance of the fall harvest that was responsible for providing sustenance over the winter. The beginning of this season was marked by the *Great Winter Feast*, a full congregation gathering with traditional food from the harvests of early America, in early December.

That evening, instead of driving across the country, Roger dined with Ron and Susan which impressed him so much, that he offered Ron a temporary position

preparing this year's holiday meals to the new congregation. Ron hadn't strayed very far from the house in Baltimore in over twenty years and Susan knew how much
this opportunity meant to Ron, so she reluctantly con-
sented. The three ate and drank well into the evening,
forging a friendship between the families. Ron was killed
soon before he was scheduled to arrive for the season.

"Mary, would you possibly be open to a recom-
mendation to replace Ron?" Susan inquired.

Mary quickly responded, "Of course I would,
Susan, I trust your opinion, especially when it comes to
your taste in culinary aptitude."

"Well, Ron has a ...family member... that has recently moved to New York after spending several years
as an apprentice to some of the finest chefs in Australia,"
Susan continued. "He is looking for work and is visiting
for the funeral. I could set up an interview if you wish."

"That would be wonderful, and more than I could
ask you to do at a time like this, thank you, Susan," Mary
replied with a grateful tone. "Have him call me tomorrow at noon, your time, to discuss the position."

"Thank you, Mary, he will be very excited," Susan
replied before ending the phone call.

Clayton slept through the evening and into the
night; the entire house was quiet shortly after midnight.
As Clayton slept, his heart began to race, and his chest

erratically rose and fell through the severe twitches of a nightmare. Clayton appeared to be back at the farmhouse, this time inside the church from his last dream. He was surrounded by empty pews in front of him, when all of a sudden, he saw the little girl quickly slip out of the church, moving past the large wooden door. Clayton called after her, "Wait, please wait!" but the little girl ran toward the house.

Clayton followed her out of the church, but he didn't see if she entered the house at all. Slowly, he walked toward the back porch near the door where he entered the kitchen from his last dream. He peered through the kitchen window and there stood Azra, talking directly to the little girl. This was the first time he could see her face, which was wracked with a terror he had never seen on anyone. Azra was pointing and yelling at her, repeating, "I am coming for you, I am stopping the Balances from getting to you, you will never be safe!"

Clayton banged on the window and Azra turned around and looked directly at him while the little girl took the opportunity to run into the basement. The look on Azra's face was distorted and evil, with a large protruding brow and bulging cheekbones that forced her eyes to have a severely sunken-in appearance, as if she was from another species, another world. This vision was so startling to Clayton that it forced him awake, now drenched in his own sweat. Realizing it was all a dream, he decided to get some water from the kitchen, as it was only down the hall from the guest bedroom where he slept. As Clayton walked to the kitchen, he could see a light already on, and he could hear faint whispering.

Clayton stopped to hear what was being said — it was Azra speaking. She was arguing with someone on the phone. "What do you mean, you don't know if it worked?" she angrily asked the person she was speaking to on the phone.

"Didn't you stick around to see if you did it right?" she continued. "You're not getting paid until I get proof!" she said with force and ended the phone call, slamming the phone down on the counter, face down.

Clayton couldn't turn around and go back to his room as the sound of him walking would be loud enough for Azra to hear, so he decided to wait a beat before entering the kitchen and act as though nothing was heard.

"Oh, hey Azra, what are you doing awake at this hour?" Clayton innocently asked her.

"Clayton, I am sorry if I woke you, I...I couldn't sleep, just thinking about mom and dad and, now...you," Azra responded, sounding unnerved and shaken by his entrance.

"No, you didn't wake me at all, I was having a nightmare and I needed some water," he replied.

"I have something better than water...here," Azra smiled, extending her arm and handing him a glass with a small amount of amber liquid in it.

"Scotch...it's my...it's *our* dad's," she corrected herself.

"Thanks," Clayton took the glass and sipped the smoothest scotch he had ever tasted.

"Whoa, that's pretty good," he smirked at Azra.

"Only the best scotch for him," she said with a slight tremor in her voice, putting on an act of sadness.

The pair talked in the kitchen, sharing their father's sixty-year old scotch, talking about their lives and getting to know one another. Azra seemed like a very private person to Clayton, and Clayton seemed like a very kind, friendly person to Azra. Throughout their conversation, Azra wished she would have chosen another room to have had her phone conversation, in the first place. She was worried she would begin to care for Clayton and needed to maintain emotional distance from him to complete her mission.

Azra knew she may need to stop him at any cost and didn't want to complicate things by thinking of him as a brother and as a friend. They both noticed the sun coming up through the kitchen window by the sink and agreed to quickly disperse to their respective rooms before Susan was awake to ask why all of the expensive scotch was gone. They hugged and parted ways for a few hours, until Susan would be calling them for breakfast.

Susan slept much later than she expected, and even after waking, she stared blankly at the ceiling, thinking about how she would be starting the rest of her life. Getting out of bed would mean she couldn't go back to the way things were when Ron was alive. She had to accept his death and she needed to carry the burden of the accident that killed her husband, as well as the accident that killed her friends so many years ago, alone. The chatter inside of her head was so loud that she forced herself out of bed and into the kitchen to make the strongest coffee of her life.

Susan noticed glasses in the sink that weren't there when she went to bed, as well as the empty bottle of Ron's scotch. This made Susan feel a bit of comfort in that it seemed the new siblings were still enjoying each other's company, even after yesterday's revelation. Susan thought that if Clayton were to accept the Donovans' offer of a job at the farm in Colorado, that Sarah may want to accompany him for support. She felt that a stronger relationship with his half-sister may keep Clayton from exposing the truth of Ron and Susan's disappearance from so long ago, that a strong connection to the family would be more important to him than getting vengeance for so many years of estrangement.

A few moments later, Azra and Clayton groggily lumbered to the kitchen after hearing Susan up and about in the house. Clayton could smell the aroma of strong, black coffee brewing and the desire to drink some was stronger than his desire to sleep, due, mainly, to the fact he hadn't been able to fall back asleep since he finished the scotch with Azra a few hours prior.

"Good morning, Clayton!" Susan said with as much

courtesy as she could muster.

"Hi, Susan, how are you feeling?" Clayton asked Susan, genuinely interested in her well-being.

"Hey, everybody," Azra joined in as she entered from the hallway.

"Clayton, there are a few things that I would like to talk to you about." Susan motioned to a seat at the kitchen table, pouring him a steaming hot, aromatic cup of fresh coffee.

"Ron was very specific in his request to provide you with a comfortable life in the event of his death," she proceeded to tell Clayton as he rubbed his tired eyes and took a sip of the coffee.

Susan continued, "I have an agreement here for you, a contract for the first installment of the portion of the estate that he wanted you to have."

Susan extended her arm and handed Clayton an agreement for a payment of five-hundred thousand dollars. Clayton saw the amount on the paper and choked on his coffee, completely surprised by this development.

"He wanted you to have half of his half of our estate, and I also have some paperwork for you to sign from the attorneys," Susan said with a quiver in her voice. She continued, "The agreement is that you receive four installments of five-hundred thousand dollars from a trust account setup in your father's name."

"It also states you will not reveal to your mother or your family, or anyone else, that Ron was your father or that he and I escaped the accident so many years ago," she continued. "You must, essentially, pretend as though you've never learned the secret we had been forced to keep all of these years."

Clayton looked at Susan with a face of bewilderment and was barely able to make enough noise to say, "I...I don't know what to say, Susan, of course you can trust me."

Susan let out a sigh of relief and laid the contract down in front of Clayton as he was too surprised to actually touch the piece of paper.

Susan continued to speak, "There is also another thing, Clayton, your father recently accepted a very important position to travel to Colorado over the holidays and be the head chef for a generous family wanting to provide holiday communion to a new congregation of their own creation."

"The family, the Donovans, built a church on their property and they want this inaugural holiday season to be very special and filled with weekly feasts from just after Thanksgiving to Christmas, and they agreed to pay Ron very handsomely," she explained further.

"I spoke to Mrs. Donovan yesterday, after the funeral, and she agreed to talk to you today at noon if you were interested in taking over the position from your father." Susan waited for a response from him.

"Uh, sure, I...I can talk to her, for sure," Clayton said as he tried to digest everything that was just thrown at him.

"I'm sorry to overload you with so much. I guess I just wanted to lay it all out there for you before too much time passed this morning," Susan apologetically confessed to Clayton, realizing she was forcing him to make so many important decisions with no notice or time to actually think about anything first.

"Um, no, Susan, it's fine, I will talk to Mrs. Donovan at noon to see if I am a good fit, and I will read through the agreement for Ron's estate as well," Clayton reassured Susan that she wasn't putting too much on him at once and noticed the concerned look on her face softening with his words.

In reality, Clayton's head was swimming with so many unanswered questions and all he really wanted to do was call his mother to tell her everything that had happened over the last twenty-four hours. He wanted to also provide for her as she was the one who suffered the most from Ron's choices. Clayton knew he would have to use an excuse for the sudden influx of money, and the job at the Donovans could be the perfect alibi for him, at least, until he thought of something more substantial.

Clayton discussed the position with Mrs. Donovan and agreed to take the place of his father. He requested a few extra days to put his affairs in order before leaving for Colorado and also asked if he could bring Azra with him to help with the planning, shopping and preparing of the weekly feasts. Azra was pleasantly surprised that Clayton thought of her before she needed to try to convince him to take her to Colorado. Everything was set now, and Azra felt her path to the Original growing clearer, as long as she stayed close to Clayton. Susan felt relieved that she weathered this storm with Clayton as she had always feared the worst. After all, Clayton had every right to refuse the agreement and expose the entire family for the mistakes of so many years ago. Clayton was also relieved and excited for his new life; he had a promising new job and more money than he ever expected. With his father's estate money, Clayton could begin the process of opening his own restaurant after he returned from Colorado in January. The future looked bright for Clayton, even after so many changes these last few weeks of his life.

CHAPTER 14 – THE DONO-VANS' PREPARATION

Ellen

Roger and Mary Donovan were anticipating the arrival of their guests, Clayton and Azra, by preparing the quarters in the barn for Clayton and the guest room in the house for Azra. Ellen was in charge of ensuring the rooms were made comfortable with fresh linens and perfectly spotless windows, mirrors and floors. Ellen spent day and night turning the empty room in the barn, that was built for an overflow of guests, into a suitable space for Clayton by hauling the spare bedframe and mattress out of the basement of the main house, cleaning it, beating the mattress free of dust, as well as assembling the entire suite in the space. The room was unpainted, so Ellen used the eggshell wall paint that was stored upstairs in her bedroom closet, to give the room the inviting appearance of cleanliness with a fresh coat of soft white paint. Clayton and Azra were coming just a few days after the Thanksgiving Day holiday, and Ellen was also in charge of creating holiday wreaths, the only holiday decoration allowed on the farm, to hang in each bedroom of the house and in the quarters of the reconstituted barn.

As Ellen twisted the vines and pine branches she gathered from the forest into round, wreath shapes, she thought about her father who had committed suicide a little over six years ago now. The pair never had much to celebrate, but Finn always decorated a Christmas tree for Ellen, and she remembered the process quite fondly. It was really the only memory left of her father, but creating these wreaths for the Donovan farm took her back to the days before her father was dead.

Ellen wondered about the people that would be staying with them, mainly if they were going to be like Mother and Father. Ellen was abused daily by the couple and was hoping that she wouldn't be even more of a target with two additional occupants of the farm. She thought about the new chef and his companion and hoped they were kind, caring people who recognized the trauma she was experiencing with the Donovans. As Ellen was finishing up her small pile of wreaths, Mother came to discuss the rules of the house now that there would be visitors over the holiday season.

"Ellen, Father and I wanted to be sure you understood the new rules of the house now that we will be hosting guests," Mother greeted Ellen with coldness, as she usually did, but with this conversation, Ellen could already tell Mother was in no mood for pleasantries.

"Yes, Mother," Ellen said, giving the full attention she had been conditioned to provide Mother when she spoke.

"As you already know, through the preparations we have asked you to make, Father and I will not be the only adults in the house for the immediate future." Mother stared at Ellen while she spoke. "You are not to discuss the family or the practices of our religion with our guests, do I make myself very clear, Ellen?" She insisted on an immediate response from Ellen by the look on her face.

"Yes, Mother, I will only speak when requested to do so," Ellen added to appease Mother.

"Ellen, you are not permitted to speak to *anyone* but Father and I, are you clear on that?" Mother inquired.

"Yes, Mother, I will not speak to anyone but you and Father while we are hosting our guests." Ellen wanted to show Mother that she was worthy of her trust.

Ellen learned that when Mother felt she was being a devout follower of the church and an obedient daughter, her physical punishments were far less severe than when she was sad, tired or displayed any semblance of disagreement.

"You will be restricted as to when you are allowed to leave your bedroom, but because we are a kind and generous family, you will be allowed to use the entirety of your room unless you are being punished," Mother informed Ellen. Ellen was excited to sleep in a bed and have the chance to gaze at the stars from her bedroom window.

Later that morning, Mother moved a small cot into Ellen's bedroom and allowed her to make the cot more comfortable with her pillow and blanket from the closet. She also brought in a very small side table with a lamp. Ellen was told these items were excessive, but necessary, as outsiders were under the silly impression that bedrooms have more than a bed in them, to give the guests the "right" impression. Mother told Ellen that those who do not follow the doctrine of the Puritan religion were not pure of mind and were easily distracted by worldly comforts, which took them further from God.

"Ellen, in order for our church to continue to survive, and to make God happy and one day be in Heaven with him, you must not do anything that could threaten our church and our plan." Mother insisted Ellen listen to this with her undivided attention. "Our practices are extreme, but they are the *correct* way, and you must never tell outsiders as they would not understand, and they will work to dismantle everything we have worked so hard to create."

With these words, Ellen started to feel the familiar chill in the air that often preceded a physical beating from Mother; she could almost predict the abuse by the cold that would creep over her body.

"Ellen, God needs to know you understand, and he needs to know we warned you properly of the consequences of your actions if you tell the visitors anything other than what we permit you to tell them, so please kneel before me," Mother said sternly.

By the time Mother had finished her sentence, Ellen was already kneeling on the cold, hard, wooden floor as she had become accustomed to the practice of being punished as a warning of possible harsher punishment. Ellen kept her gaze ahead of herself, staring at Mother's legs while Mother created fists with both hands. One after the other, Mother struck the top of Ellen's skull with her fists, counting, until she reached ten strikes to her soft, blonde hair and scalp. There was a soft, bloody patch in the center of Ellen's head that hadn't completely healed from her last punishment, making it more painful than usual. Mother demanded that Ellen get to her feet to see if she now fully understood the seriousness of Mother's request to remain silent during the visit of the new chef and his companion. As Ellen began to stand from her kneeling position, she could feel her body shaking with the nausea that often accompanied this kind of punishment. Ellen stood on her left leg first, and then the right, which buckled underneath her, and she fell to the ground, losing consciousness for a brief moment. Mother picked Ellen up by her hair, which forced her out of her barely lucid state and back onto her feet to finish the punishment.

"I now fully understand the seriousness of your request, Mother. Thank you for showing me the truth," Ellen responded with blood shot eyes and a slight slur to her words.

"You are quite welcome, Ellen, now please go wash the blood from your hair. God doesn't like to see your weakness," Mother softly said to Ellen while she fought back tears of her own.

Occasionally, Mother would go too far with her punishments, even by her own standards, and accidently show Ellen that she, too, suffered during these sacrificial displays of devoutness to God. Mother explained to Ellen that she would also need to use the same force with her children, if she was ever chosen to marry and have children by an older male member of the congregation. Seeing Mother's tears brought Ellen small comforts even when she was being brutally attacked, now that she had grown used to the severity of the training.

Ellen slowly made her way to the washroom to clean her head wounds and be presentable to God. The sting of the cold water, the only temperature of water in the house, snapped Ellen out of her lethargy and provided her with the fortitude to carry on for the rest of the day, cleaning, decorating and preparing for the guests that were expected to arrive first thing the next morning. Before bed, Mother came to visit with Ellen as she was getting ready to spend her first night outside of her closet.

As Mother entered the room, Ellen prepared for what she assumed was another reminder of the punishment that may be in store for her if she were to violate the order she was given not to speak to the guests. Instead, Mother sat Ellen down on the cot and held her as she audibly wept. Ellen was taken aback by this, as Mother had never shown her this kind of affection before this night and was nervous for what to expect next. Minutes passed as Mother continued to hold Ellen and cry, until they both fell asleep in one another's arms.

That night, Ellen dreamt of a farmhouse with rooms of bright yellow and gold wallpaper with a warm, summer glow that filled the house. In the dream, Ellen felt more comfortable and safer than she had ever felt in her life prior to this dream.

The next morning, Ellen woke up alone, in her cot, in the bedroom of the farmhouse. Mother came to her door and told Ellen to be ready for further instructions once the guests arrived, but to make sure that she only came out of her room after she is permitted to do so. She was to read her scriptures, recite them in the afternoon for Mother, and perform the tasks that are presented to her each morning. Ellen reassured Mother that she understood, and Mother left her to prepare for the day by getting dressed and going downstairs for breakfast before the guests' arrival.

Ellen knew that Mother's behavior last night was not an invitation to begin to expect affection from her, but she couldn't help but wonder what made her react that way. Ellen began to understand that being *human* was a shared experience regardless of how hard some people tried to hide it from others.

CHAPTER 15 – THE DONOVANS' GUESTS

C layton and Azra traveled back to New York together to pack their essentials and take care of any
outstanding debts or commitments. Clayton wanted to
give Scott enough money to cover the rent through Feb-
ruary and Azra needed to remove her belongings from
the sublet she had been renting. Clayton told Azra she
could keep her things in his bedroom during their nine-
week stay in Colorado, and even discussed the possibility
of moving in with him once they returned. Clayton was
much wealthier now that he had received the first installment of part of his father's estate, and he was eager
to share it with his half-sister, someone he never even
knew existed just a few short weeks ago. Azra and Clayton had a unique relationship and he saw her as someone
he could trust, even though they hadn't really known
each other for that long. Azra told Clayton very little
about her past, and he felt it was best to allow her to
share with him when she felt comfortable doing so.

After the pair bid farewell to Scott, they headed to
the airport for a direct flight to Denver and then a shorter
flight to a smaller, regional airport near the Donovan

farm. Clayton asked Mr. Donovan about renting a car, but he insisted against it as he was expecting Clayton to be available anytime he was requested and couldn't have him absent from the farm, for any reason. Clayton conceded to this request as he was being paid quite well, and, after all, he was only staying for a little over two months. Azra was confused and a bit concerned after Clayton shared that Mr. Donovan was adamant against them renting a car from the airport, and she realized there may be more to this experience than what she, or Clayton, expected. Clayton told Azra she was being overly cautious and the family was just very conservative. He tried to reassure her they were just safeguarding the first holiday season at their new church.

As the plane took off from New York City, Azra's eyelids began to droop and she was asleep faster than anyone else on the plane. Clayton was grateful for the time alone; in fact, he was quite nervous for this unique opportunity and wanted to just sit in the silence of his own thoughts for a moment before others would be expecting more of him. Over the last few weeks, he discovered that his father had been alive for the last twenty-five years, was very wealthy, and had a wife and daughter in America. For all intents and purposes, Clayton was living a completely different life because he had found his father, his stepmother, and his half-sister.

Azra's head fell on Clayton's shoulder about an hour into the flight and she began to mumble in her sleep.

He didn't want to disturb her, at first, but as she continued to sleep, she started to speak more and more.

"Can you hear me; can anyone hear me?" Azra said while she slept. "She's taken over and I can't get out of here, help me get out of here," she continued to say, over and over. "Help me, save me from her before it's too late for me," Azra said before Clayton decided to wake her.

"Azra, you are having a bad dream and shouting in your sleep," he nudged her, trying to keep from making even more of a scene on the quiet flight.

"Oh my God, I am sorry, was I really loud?" she responded as she regained consciousness and looked around to see if anyone was looking at her.

"Yeah, you just kept asking someone to save you from *her*," Clayton answered. "You must have been having a nightmare."

"Yeah, I...I guess I was," Azra agreed while knowing full well it was Sarah calling out while she wasn't paying attention.

"Are you okay?" Clayton asked with genuine concern.

"Oh, yeah, just still out of it, is all," she smiled at Clayton, hoping he didn't suspect anything about Sarah. Azra also realized she needed to talk to Sarah soon to keep her from ruining the plans to find the Original. She was certain that Clayton was taking her in the right direction. The coincidences were just too great, and she was determined to ensure that he stay in the dark regarding her plans until she had no choice but to reveal them to him, most likely right before she would have to kill him.

Azra's goals hadn't changed as she got closer to Clayton and she knew if Sarah got involved, that she wouldn't allow Azra to complete the mission of the Imbalance. Her entire existence revolved around this goal. She represented the Imbalance within Sarah, the change in the tide of the Legacy, one that represented the fall of humanity and the end of a species undeserving of its place in the Universe. Azra made her way to the back of plane to wait for the restroom. Once she got inside, she called for Sarah, hoping she was willing to talk to her, "Sarah, it's me, we need to talk."

"Is it really you?" Sarah responded with the desperation of someone locked away against her will. "Why have you done this to me, what is going on?" Sarah demanded answers to why she was being silenced.

"Listen, Sarah, I don't have time to explain everything right now, I just need you to trust me and understand that what I am doing is the *right* thing." Azra wanted to try to talk to Sarah as her friend and her ally, the way she used to do.

"Please return as soon as you can, I feel a change in you and in us," Sarah pleaded.

"I will, I promise, but you have to stay quiet while I sleep!" she demanded.

"I promise," Sarah said with a quiver in her voice.

Sarah had spent the last few weeks as a prisoner

in her own mind while Azra took full control over her life. Sarah knew that she recently visited her childhood home in Baltimore, but Azra kept her in the dark the entire time. She also saw her traveling companion, Clayton, but wasn't aware that he was her half-brother or that her father had passed away in a tragic accident. Azra had no plans on letting Sarah take back control over her own body and mind. She was being led by forces stronger than Sarah's will-power, by her position as the Imbalance who was chosen to end the Legacy that had been maintaining human existence on Earth.

After the four-hour flight, the two arrived where Mr. Donovan was waiting for them. Clayton and Azra exited the small airport and saw a man with a sign reading, "Donovan Farm." The man holding the sign was a much smaller, unassuming figure than either of them expected. Mr. Donovan was attractive enough for an older man, but no more than five and a half feet tall, and he was quite thin with a pale, sallow complexion. He had a pleasant look on his face, and this immediately put Clayton, and especially Azra, at ease. "See what I told you, just nice people who want things to be perfect," said Clayton, nudging her.

"Not so fast, detective, you can't judge a book by its extremely *plain* cover," Azra retorted as they both giggled while they walked toward their host.

Mr. Donovan drove an old Honda Accord sedan, not exactly what Clayton had in mind with the generous salary that he was being paid for his services, yet it was something else that helped ease his anxiety about the job he was hired to do. On the ride from the small airport to the farm, Mr. Donovan asked his guests to call him Roger. Clayton and Azra agreed and they exchanged pleasant conversation for the duration of the ride. Mr. Donovan thought twice about bringing up Ron's accident, as suggested by Mrs. Donovan, but he offered a simple gesture of his condolences, which Clayton was quite thankful for as he really wouldn't know what to say to a stranger about his relationship with his estranged father. He and Azra politely thanked Mr. Donovan and responded, "I appreciate the opportunity that you gave me to honor him this way."

The car began to climb the uphill, gravel driveway to the Donovan farm. The trio was discussing the differences in the weather between the east coast and Colorado, when the farmhouse came into view. Clayton was laughing and about to remind Azra that she needed to drink enough water in this higher altitude and much drier climate, when he was completely struck by what he was seeing. The plain, tragic farmhouse of his dreams was creeping closer and closer as the car made its way up the driveway.

"You ok, Clayton?" Mr. Donovan asked as Clayton just simply stopped talking and stared at the house with his mouth wide-open.

"Oh, yeah, I'm fine, Roger," Clayton responded,

thinking of how weird it would sound if he told Mr. Donovan his house was a thing right out of his own nightmares.

Clayton started to feel his heart race and palms become clammy. Azra looked at Clayton, feeling as though she realized what was going on with him. Judging by the look on his face, as well as his actions, she knew they were in the right place. Azra knew this was where everything was about to change. The car came to a stop in front of the house where Mr. Donovan began to get the luggage out of the trunk. Clayton got out of the back seat, looked up at the house, and there she was, in her window as she was in his dreams. They locked eyes with one another, and Clayton flashed an awkward smile and offered a slight wave to Ellen. Ellen took her eyes off Clayton and saw that Father had also noticed her presence in the window.

Ellen immediately disappeared from the window as Mother had made it very clear, the night before, that she was to always remain hidden from the guests unless she was specifically called upon by Mother or Father. Azra also saw the little girl in the window and wondered who she was and why she was so influential to Clayton. Was this little girl the Original referenced in the letter? Was this who she needed to kill, a *child*?

As they moved toward the house with their luggage, Azra was silent as she thought about the tasks at hand. Clearly, this place was important to Clayton, as he was making apparent with each passing minute since they arrived from the airport. His speech was short and blunt, his facial expressions were blank, and his complexion grew colorless, as if he had seen a ghost. Azra needed to make sure that she found the person that was truly the Original and would need an elaborate plan to take care of both the Original as well as Clayton. The farm and church hosted many people several times a week and Azra would need to study everyone that walked through the doors of this place. First, though, she needed to check on one outstanding task she had set in motion prior to leaving Baltimore for New York, and then, New York for Colorado.

Azra checked her cell phone and noticed she didn't have service on the farm. She asked Mr. Donovan if she could connect to their Wi-Fi access to make a call, to which he replied, "Oh, I am so sorry, Sarah, but we are slowly moving away from technology and other modern-day conveniences to get closer to God, our creator."

"I completely understand, Roger, do you happen to have a telephone that I may use in the house?" Azra politely asked her host.

"Yes, of course, Sarah, let me show you the way," Mr. Donovan responded. He called her Sarah as that was the name she was using as the two families became familiar with one another. Azra didn't go to the trouble of correcting him, and drawing more attention to the matter, so she simply responded to him when he addressed her as such.

Azra was led inside, followed by Clayton who was trying very hard not to make it obvious he had been there before, in his dreams. The décor was exactly as he dreamt. The floor creaked in the same places and even the slight chill in the air was present, milder, but still present. Clayton understood that he was asleep each time he visited this house, but he couldn't believe that everything was just as he remembered it from the dreams. "How is this possible?" he quietly asked himself so no one would hear him.

"How is *what* possible?" Clayton heard a woman's voice behind him, coming from the kitchen, as she quickly walked to greet the guests.

"How...how is this place so beautiful?" he quickly responded to Mrs. Donovan as she gave Clayton an inquisitive look.

Mrs. Donovan was tall and thin with very strong facial features. She had a natural downturn to her mouth that seemed as though she was always frowning. She introduced herself as "Mrs. Donovan" and took their luggage from them. Her walk was unmistakable as the sound of her heavy footsteps filled the mostly empty house.

"So, is it just the three of you, then?" Clayton asked Mrs. Donovan as she fumbled with their bags.

"The three of us...yes...it is just the *three* of us," Mrs. Donovan responded with a very pointed monotone, but added, "Although, there are always people coming and going around here, it's so hard to find any time to your-self!" Her tone had changed, with the second comment, and she placed the bags down in the front room of the house.

"If you will excuse me for one second, I need to check on the linens for your room in the barn, Clayton, but Mr. Donovan will show you around the farm as well as where you will be preparing the meals while you are here," Mrs. Donovan said in a hurry as she made her way up the stairs, her hard-heeled shoes stomping out her exact location every step of the way.

Mr. Donovan showed Azra to the phone in the kit-chen, and he made his way back to Clayton to give her privacy for her phone call. Azra dialed the number from her cell phone contacts list and placed the receiver up to her ear.

"Hey, it's me," Azra said after the person on the other end answered the phone.

"Is he dead?"

...

"How did you get back into the room?"

...

"Oh...well, did anyone see you go back?"

...

"Are you *positive* that he's dead?"

...

"Ok, yeah, of course I believe you, I'm just on edge lately, and I was worried."

...

"Great, I won't be able to talk for a few months, so lay low and you should be receiving the check in a few days, I've already sent it."

...

"Same to you, Fawad, I understand why you needed the job done, you didn't need him holding that over your head for the rest of your life, so we both had our reasons."

...

"I'm just glad that you agreed with me, you know he would have eventually gone to the police."

...

"Well, I knew that you had a price, we all do."

...

"You will have to deal with her yourself, Fawad, she's your sister-in-law, she was warned to know her place."

...

"Not sure, she must've had someone looking for her."

...

"Johanna...I mean, *Azra*, won't be bothering you any longer, she confessed to the murder in the alley and is in New York, serving her sentence in a state facility."

...

"Yeah, no way she will be getting out anytime soon."

...

"Get rid of your sister-in-law, she's the only piece of the puzzle that hasn't been taken care of at this point, and it was her *choice* to write Ameer that letter."

...

"I will check in after the new year."

...

Azra hung up the phone, breathing a heavy sigh of relief.

After Johanna confessed everything to Sarah, the night she was arrested, Azra did her research at the library the next day, during the letter translation, and saw that Ameer had survived the accident in Hong Kong. After finding out her place in the Legacy through the letter, Azra needed to know the status of Ameer's recovery.

Azra contacted the hospital where Ameer was in the Intensive Care Unit, posing as his mother, and the hospital informed her that she was the only person from Ameer's family that had bothered to inquire about him. Azra mentioned that she was divorced from Ameer's father and asked for his contact information, stating she may have better luck contacting him. Luckily, the hospital was able to retrieve Ameer's father's phone number from Ameer's cell phone and they never even questioned Azra's story's authenticity.

Azra alerted Fawad of the accident, but only because she needed him to help eliminate the threat of Ameer possibly getting in the way of her plan. She told Fawad that she was aware of what he did to his wife so many years ago but would keep this knowledge to herself if he was willing to help her. She asked him to go to Hong Kong and kill Ameer in his hospital bed in exchange for the same amount of money that he made for selling his wife to the gang from South Africa. She reminded him that it was in his best interest to follow her request as Ameer would most likely go to the police once he had recovered anyway, plus the incentive of the money was to ensure that he was motivated to actually do the job, correctly.

What Fawad wasn't aware of, though, was that Azra was documenting the conversation using a small voice recorder and would isolate the section of the call when Fawad outlined exactly what he did to kill Ameer and how he was sure that he was dead. She would keep this information just in case she needed to blackmail Fawad in the future.

CHAPTER 16 – AZRA'S OPPORTUNITY

Johanna was initially drawn to Sarah, because of the name "Azra," so it was obvious that Ameer had ties to the Legacy that could impede Azra's mission, and this was just too timely to be a coincidence, as was meeting Clayton. Azra knew she was being shown things that were only meant for the Balances and for the Original to see. Ameer had to be the other Balance and Azra needed to deal with him. The Legacy was putting her in the middle of all of this for a reason, and that reason was to ensure that the Legacy failed. Even if she was wrong about Ameer, she knew she couldn't be too cautious.

Azra walked into the front room where Clayton and Mr. Donovan were talking about Clayton's preferred preparation of deep-frying a turkey, something Mr. Donovan always wanted to try.

"Right, well, let's have a tour, shall we?" Mr. Donovan said before taking the two on a walking tour of the property.

Clayton was worried for the little girl he saw in the window, and judging by Mrs. Donovan's reaction, he felt as though he had good reason to be worried. Clayton spent the entire tour of his new, temporary home thinking about how he was going to try and talk to the little girl.

"Roger, do you have a daughter?" Clayton innocently brought her up as they walked toward the church so that Clayton could see his room.

"You must be talking about our sweet Ellen," Mr. Donovan responded. "We adopted the poor child who started her short life off far from the mercy of God."

"I would love to meet her," Clayton commented.

Mr. Donovan looked at him and then at Azra and responded, "Yes, of course, you will have plenty of time to meet Ellen as well as the entire congregation; they will all be arriving soon so I can make a formal announcement in the church this afternoon."

The entire congregation was coming to the church to meet Clayton and Azra as their guests for the next nine weeks. Mr. Donovan asked Clayton to mingle with the congregation to get an idea of foods to incorporate into the holiday festivities; foods that he knew people would enjoy and would give them a bit more of a reason to come to church. Mr. Donovan laughed at his own insinuation that people weren't planning on coming to church. "Actually, church services are a completely mandatory part of our congregation, excused absences are only issued for extreme and unforeseen circumstances."

Clayton wasn't sure how to react to that statement, as he had never heard of any church that would throw you out of its congregation for simply not coming to each and every service, so he just half-smiled, hoping not to make his discomfort obvious.

After the entire property was toured, led by Mr. Donovan, Clayton took his bags and decided to take some time to rest and freshen up before the gathering this evening. Azra was shown to the spare room on the second floor of the farmhouse, the floor that was also shared by Mr. and Mrs. Donovan's bedrooms as well as Ellen's bedroom. She placed her things on the floor of the mostly empty room. The bed in the room was just a small cot, but Azra didn't mind the meager accommodations. This wasn't about her comfort; this was about fulfilling her destiny. Just as Azra was changing into her robe to rest before the afternoon and evening gathering, her thoughts were interrupted by the singing of a child.

Azra peered out of her bedroom door and looked toward the singing. She could see into another room where she spotted a little girl standing in front of one of her bedroom windows, just looking at the world outside her walls. She was standing completely still and lightly humming a soft melody. The girl was facing away from Azra, and she could see nothing other than the little girl's back.

Azra stepped up to the doorway of the room and introduced herself to the girl, "Hi there, what's your name? I'm Sarah, but you can call me Azra," she said with a slight hesitation and waited for the girl to acknowledge her existence.

"Hello there, are you Ellen?" she spoke again, to try and capture the girl's attention.

"You said to call you Azra?" the little girl said sweetly to Azra, without turning around to look at her.

"Yes, that's right…Azra," she replied.

"Azra is a bad name," the child responded, in a dream-like, childish way.

"How can a name be *bad*?" said Azra, with an attempt to lighten the conversation into a more familiar tone.

"Your name isn't Azra, Sarah," she stated in a matter-of-fact tone, "The name that you use belongs to another, someone you have betrayed."

Just then, the door to Ellen's room softly closed in Azra's face, without severity or violence; it simply closed with just enough force for the latch to click into place. Azra didn't try to stop it, mostly due to her surprise that it was moving at all, but also with the understanding that Ellen seemed to be letting Azra know that she was aware of who she was and why she was there.

As Azra turned to walk back down the hallway, she heard a painful scream come from Ellen's room. Azra tried to open the door, but the doorknob was just spinning and spinning, and the door wouldn't budge an inch. Azra panicked and gripped the spinning doorknob as the cries from the child began growing more and more muffled as though someone was suffocating her. Azra shouted for someone to help her as her attempts to open the door were failing. Mrs. Donovan heard Azra calling for help and ran toward the stairs leading to the second-floor bedrooms. Just as Mrs. Donovan was reaching the stairs from the kitchen, Ellen's door opened with a force of its own and Azra stood there, bewildered, in front of an empty room.

Just as Azra began to peer deeper into the room, Ellen, Mr. Donovan, and Clayton entered the house through the front door, close to the bottom of the stairs where Mrs. Donovan was standing.

"Sarah, do you need something?" Mrs. Donovan shouted up the stairs as the trio entered and began wondering what was going on in the house.

"No, thank you, I thought I heard something, but I guess my mind is just playing tricks on me," Azra responded, knowing she couldn't just come out with what happened if she wanted to keep suspicions low from the Donovans or from Clayton.

"Sarah, could you come downstairs for a moment, I would like you to meet our daughter, Ellen," Mr. Donovan called from downstairs, standing behind Mrs. Donovan.

"Sure, be right there," Azra replied with hesitation due to what just occurred upstairs.

Azra made her way to the first floor of the farmhouse and could hear the voices of the Donovans and Clayton in the kitchen. As she walked toward the kitchen, she could see the back of the little girl again, between where Azra stood and the others in the kitchen. As Azra moved closer to the kitchen, Ellen turned around, and introduced herself to Azra. "Hello, Sarah, I am Ellen, it is such a pleasure to meet you," Ellen said with a great deal of politeness and completely precise diction.

"Um, hi, it's also a pleasure to meet you, Ellen," Azra replied to the greeting from the girl.

"Are you finding everything suitable with your room, is there anything I can get you so that you are more comfortable while you stay here at our farm?" Ellen inquired of Azra, making her feel slightly uncomfortable.

"Oh, no, Ellen, you have already made me feel very comfortable, thank you," Azra responded while looking at Ellen and wondering why she was speaking to her as though she was a customer of *Hotel* Donovan.

As Azra was meeting Ellen, she could see the Donovans talking to Clayton; they were highly engaged with their discussion planning the *Great Winter Feast* that would be taking place a little over two weeks from now. Azra decided to use this opportunity to see if she could get to know Ellen with more than a simple pleasantry.

"Ellen, tell me, how do you like living here in Colorado? It seems like such a beautiful place to grow up," Azra said with a smile.

"Yes, God certainly did make this an ideal place for us to spread the word of his glory." Ellen sounded a bit like a pre-recorded message that was responding exactly the way the Donovans coached her to respond.

"Ellen, are you happy living here with the Dono-vans? Do they treat you well?" Azra wanted to see how Ellen would respond to this inquiry. The letter stated the Original would be living a life of great sadness and tra-gedy and Azra wanted to gauge Ellen's responses.

"Mother and Father treat me as any parent should treat a child," Ellen answered. "I have many challenges, but Mother said that I will be rewarded in Heaven for my sacrifices here on Earth; it is written in the doctrine of our religion."

Azra couldn't judge Ellen by this response. If she was anywhere else, in any other situation, she would think this was a peculiar way for a child to describe life at home with their parents, but in this household, and with such religiously devout parents, she couldn't tell if Ellen was being mistreated or if this was simply the lot of all children in her situation.

Azra and Clayton were not given any real details about the church or its practices, and Azra was slightly concerned with meeting the congregation today not knowing, at all, what to expect. The first of the congre-gation members started to arrive as Azra finished her conversation with Ellen. The cars slowly crept their way up the long driveway and, one by one, the families exited their vehicles, neatly clothed in their plain suits and dresses and filed into the barn for the service. Mrs. Dono-van glanced at Ellen, paused, then said, "Ellen, please show Sarah upstairs, and the both of you, get prepared for church."

Azra wasn't used being told what to do, but the preconditioned obedience instilled by Sarah's mother was still very present, even if Sarah's consciousness was locked away and unable to make decisions or perform actions. She followed Ellen upstairs and made her way to her bedroom to change for service. Mrs. Donovan followed the pair, a few paces behind, and knocked on Azra's door.

"Sarah, I have your service dress ready for you," Mrs. Donovan called to Azra from the other side of the door.

"Oh, that's ok, Mrs. Donovan, I haven't worn a dress since my kindergarten graduation," responded Azra in the most polite tone that she could muster.

"Sarah, our congregation has rules and the attire you wear during your presence at each service is one of the most important rules. If you are not able to wear the dress, you will not be permitted in the church during the service, and if you are not present at the services, your presence will not be needed here at the farm," Mrs. Donovan calmly, but sternly, retorted.

"Um...sure, ok, Mrs. Donovan, I am sorry if I offended you," Azra tried to immediately diffuse the situation after noticing the slight change in her voice.

"Sarah, it may seem silly to you, to be so particular in matters of our religion, but this is our purpose here on

Earth, you have to understand *why* we would be so insistent." Mrs. Donovan asked Azra to consider her side of the issue.

"Well, of course I do, I have the same convictions, Mrs. Donovan, I will happily wear the dress and I will honor your requests while I am here on the farm," Azra conceded to Mrs. Donovan, thinking about her own purpose for coming to the farm with Clayton, to find the Original and fulfill her own destiny.

The dress was a deep, cherry red, and made of a very stiff cotton. It was not a form fitting dress, by design, but did provide warmth for the chilly November air in Colorado. All the women and girls would be wearing the exact same dress, the only variance was in the color, a solid, primary color. Mrs. Donovan's dress was the same, as well, with the exception of a simple, white collar that was attached to the neck of the dress. This made Mrs. Donovan look as if she held an important position within the church, which she did, as an Elder.

Mr. Donovan was the Deacon and an Elder and, so far, the Donovans were the only Elders of the congregation. Mr. Donovan informed Clayton and Azra that they were appointing two more Elders to serve the church and were moving their particular denomination into a more inclusive environment by allowing women to serve as Elders. Mr. Donovan saw a woman's duty and privilege of bearing children to be of great value to making important decisions that impacted the church and the community.

Azra finished getting ready for the service and met Clayton and the Donovans downstairs before making their way to the barn. "The *New Order of Modern-Day Puritans* has been our dream for many years, and adopting Ellen was the beginning of our work for God." Mr. Donovan continued, "This child was selected by God to be saved, but she was on a path selected by evil; we knew that we had to intervene. Mrs. Donovan knew that Ellen was special from the very first day we welcomed her into our home," Mr. Donovan said with pride as he looked toward his wife.

"It wasn't hard to see that Ellen was special, that she was meant to do great things, but was plagued with the *devil's influence*," Mrs. Donovan interjected.

Azra's interest was piqued with these words and questioned, "What do you mean by the '*devil's influence*'?"

Mrs. Donovan interrupted Mr. Donovan as he was about to answer her question. "Ellen, without our intervention and the teachings of our religion, would have been a dangerous and evil force on Earth. We believe that without conversion to the Puritan religion, Ellen would have continued to wreak havoc upon the Earth and be a true embodiment of evil."

"Ellen killed her parents, separately years apart from one another, and it was her existence, alone, that was to blame; evil simply followed her wherever she went," Mr. Donovan added.

Clayton and Azra stood there, listening to their story, and tried to disguise their disbelief that such a sweet, little girl could be compared to the anti-Christ. Clayton remembered his dreams, and just how sad Ellen was in them. He also recalled the message, "I'm waiting", that she sent him. Azra felt this story was just a misunderstanding by religious fanatics as they weren't able to understand Ellen's true destiny as an Original in the Legacy. This worked for Azra, though, and gave her an idea about how to approach Ellen. She would convince the family to allow her to get closer to the child, to determine if she truly was what Azra suspected. Azra was going to work to convince the Donovans, Clayton, as well as the congregation, that she was interested in the conversion to Puritanism and ask to be involved in Ellen's "salvation".

Azra decided to wait until tomorrow to discuss this with Mrs. Donovan, using tonight's service as the main subject of her conversation. If Azra's plan went well, she would be given more than sufficient access to Ellen and, before too long, would be able to determine if she needed to be eliminated to stop the Legacy of her time.

CHAPTER 17 – FAWAD'S CHOICES

Fawad, in his own guilty mind, had no choice but to follow the demands of Azra. Johanna confessed everything to Sarah (before Azra completely took over), which included her entire story that started with her days at the hospital. Her tragic beginnings were marked as a trafficked woman, betrayed by her husband, and left for dead in the hands of a violent and notorious gang.

Wife selling in Pakistan was now a crime, possibly punishable by death, but was once a common practice when families were faced with starvation due to extreme poverty or when she dishonored her husband. The sale of women in exchange for money still occurs in Pakistan, but it must be done under secrecy, like other crimes against women such as mercy killings. If Azra revealed Fawad's betrayal of his wife, he (and his brothers) would certainly be imprisoned through the corroboration of his sister-in-law's testimony. His sister-in-law, wife of his eldest brother, was treated very poorly by her husband and would be more than *motivated* to provide all of the evidence needed to incriminate the entire family. She knew everything about Johanna's abduction and began looking for her, many years ago.

Azra contacted Fawad, using her birth name "Sarah," and bribed Fawad to kill his son, Ameer. Knowing that he could leverage his brother's influence to possibly silence his sister-in-law in secret, she offered him a monetary incentive to follow through with her request. The fear of being imprisoned and possibly killed, accompanied with the moderate sum of money, was too much for Fawad to ignore. Azra also had to be careful about using the name "Azra", to ensure Fawad wouldn't be suspicious of her intentions. There was no way he would know about the Legacy and if she used his wife's name, he may become suspicious of her intentions and, quite possibly, her sanity.

Fawad never actually expected to have to kill his son. Ameer had been in serious condition and it wasn't until his doctor began discussing taking Ameer out of his medically induced coma, that Fawad needed to plan a way to kill Ameer and make it look like he died due to hospital negligence.

The night after discussing the process of bringing Ameer out of the coma, he noticed a nurse adding morphine to his IV bag. That gave Fawad the idea to use the morphine to kill Ameer and no one would suspect that his own father, who grieved daily over his son as he lay unconscious in a coma, would also want him dead. As the nurse was preparing the syringe to add to the IV bag, he could see she added a full syringe of the liquid that she drew from the vial of morphine. When the nurse returned the next day to prepare more morphine, as Ameer was being revived from his coma, Fawad asked the nurse if she could get him a basin, as he was pretending to feel nauseous. The nurse quickly dropped the morphine and the syringe, and left the room to retrieve the basin.

Fawad took two syringes from the cabinet where he had seen the nurse retrieve them, filled them both with morphine, and placed them in his pocket. The vial was relatively large, and he hoped the nurse wouldn't notice the missing liquid. She arrived with the basin and Fawad thanked her politely but smiled and told her it must have been a false alarm. The nurse smiled back at him and told him to keep the small, plastic basin by his side, "just in case." Fawad laughed and promised her that he would. The nurse added the single dose of morphine and left the room.

Fawad, sat and observed his son, and hesitated to deliver the lethal doses of morphine while Ameer lay still in his coma. He remembered the son he raised, with fondness and pride, even when Ameer was disobedient. Accidently, he drifted off to sleep during this contemplation, but was disturbed a few hours later by Ameer coming out of his coma, leading to the confrontation about the letter Ameer discovered, which drove Fawad out of the room. A few hours later, the nurse came back to deliver more pain medicine which caused Ameer to drift back asleep. Fawad was right outside of Ameer's room, secretly observing, and entered to deliver the medication that would soon stop his heart from beating. The nurse would later be fired for negligence and no one would ever suspect Fawad of foul play.

Fawad arrived home two days after his conversation with Azra and called on his older brother to come to the house. The men discussed the events of the last few weeks, of which his brother was totally unaware, and arranged to have his sister-in-law, collected the next morning while she slept, much in the same way as Fawad's wife was abducted so many years ago. Women were being trafficked just as much now as they were twenty-five years ago, but Fawad's sister-in-law was no longer a young woman, so the monetary compensation was much less than the men expected. Regardless, the plan was carried out, even with the knowledge that she would be used primarily for slave labor and, most likely, die from severe abuse and starvation. Azra's plan was working, and soon, would be complete.

As discussed in the letter that was intercepted by Johanna, and later stolen by Azra, one of the Balances was destined to die before discovering their life's purpose. Ameer was a Balance, and he died not knowing his purpose. Azra knew that eliminating Ameer could help to ensure that the Balance never reached the Original. She was fighting against her own cause in the process, as one of the two Balances was destined to die to save the human race. Azra was eliminating a Balance, to possibly stop both from intercepting the Original, while simultaneously doing the work for the Legacy by ending the life of a Balance.

Azra wasn't alone in her position; Johanna was also an Imbalance, but she was still functioning as the Legacy had intended, as far as the fate of the Imbalance was concerned. Her entire life was a gauge of the state of humanity, and as the species fell further and further from the grace of protecting the planet, as well as itself, each Legacy's pair of Imbalances would live more and more tragic lives. These tragic experiences would, one day, reach a tipping point, eventually forcing the Imbalances to serve their final role of stopping the Legacy from fulfilling its purpose. Imbalances would only be relieved of their suffering when the Original received the message from the Balance and learned to love again, to trust again, and to live again.

Johanna had been living in a high-security state institution in New York after confessing everything she had experienced from the day she was admitted to the hospital in South Africa, through her travels to Hong Kong and New York City. Life in the institution was restrictive and cold, but Johanna had been living so long with the pain and questions surrounding her early life that she didn't seem to really even notice that she was, essentially, in prison. To her, she was stable, clean, and no longer taking copious amounts of drugs to simply fall asleep. She was still experiencing the torturous mood swings of high elation one minute and then a hollow, sickening feeling of sorrow, the next. The doctors at the institution diagnosed Johanna with *Manic Depressive Disorder* and tried to explain the mood swings through psychological terms and symptoms, and they almost seemed to fit, but nothing ever worked to curb her suffering. The medicine made her drowsy, made her barely alert, but she would still *feel*.

After a few weeks in the custody of the New York Department of Justice and the State Department of Mental Health, Johanna received a visitor. Smitty, the detective she met the night Azra called the police after Johanna's confession to Sarah about her entire ordeal, had news for Johanna and wanted to discuss it in person. Smitty's first name was Angela, and she had a soft spot for abused women, one of the reasons she was interested in law enforcement in the first place.

After Johanna's arrest, Smitty dove into her story to get as much background information as she could, so she could fully understand what happened to Johanna, since she really didn't seem to know, herself. Smitty was able to track down her nurse at the hospital in South Africa through a channel she had here in the United States, and because of that relationship, the nurse agreed to talk about Johanna. Smitty told the nurse that anything she would tell her would be totally confidential and that she was trying to help Johanna get out of "some trouble" here in the states. With the abduction story corroborated, Smitty also wanted to investigate the young man that Johanna said was chasing her right before he was hit by a bus in front of her hotel.

"Johanna, tell me how much you remember about the young man that was chasing you and calling out with the name, Azra." Smitty looked directly into her eyes and asked her to revisit that day in Hong Kong.

"Well, there isn't much to remember about him, I mean, he got out of a cab and started running toward me without looking to see if the road was clear," Johanna responded, not understanding why Smitty was asking her to relive an event that she would rather forget.

"I looked into the young man, and he was accidently killed the same night he came out of a medically induced coma. His doctor placed him in a coma so he could properly heal from his internal injuries," Smitty said while making constant eye contact with Johanna.

"Oh, dear, he actually lived through that horrific accident? He looked so broken." Johanna started to cry.

"Yes, he did, but his nurse accidentally gave him too much morphine the night he woke up. But that's not what I came here to tell you, Johanna." Smitty swallowed very hard, trying to hide the fact that she was not looking forward to finishing what she had to say.

"The young man's name was Ameer Baqri and he was a teacher living in Pakistan. Ameer had a mother that went missing when he was seven years old and he was twenty-nine years old when he died, just two weeks ago. Johanna, Ameer's mother's name was Azra Baqri and here is a picture of what she looked like twenty-two years ago," Smitty handed Johanna a picture of a younger woman, one that looked like it could have been Johanna's younger sister.

Johanna looked at the picture and the memories of her abduction came rushing into her head as clear as if she was watching them on television. She gripped the sides of the table where she and Smitty were sitting and tried to speak, but all she could do was scream. Johanna remembered what happened the evening she was brutally abducted and remembered who orchestrated everything, her husband. The abductors didn't know the cotton hood they placed on her head had a tear in it and Johanna could see her husband counting the rupees as she was dragged from the house.

"Ameer, oh my Ameer," Johanna said as she remembered who he was.

"Yes, Johanna, Ameer was your son, and he was trying to find you, and your real name is Azra," Smitty tearfully explained to Johanna.

Both women were crying at the meeting table and Smitty gave Johanna the support that she could tell she needed. The two women sat there, in an embrace, while Johanna wept for her son, the handsome young man she saw for only a brief moment before he was brutally thrown into a parked car by that city bus.

"Johanna, the US Embassy worked with Hong Kong to keep you in this country as long as you were in our custody. If you help me, I can ensure that Pakistani officials hold your husband, Fawad, accountable and that he is no longer a threat to you. You could return to Pakistan to be with the rest of your family after we work to get a reduced sentence on your manslaughter charge," Smitty said while squeezing Johanna's hands tighter than she realized.

"I can go *back* to Pakistan?" Johanna asked with a surprised look on her face. She continued, "I, I just don't know what to do."

Smitty gave her a look of understanding and patience, "We will only do what you are comfortable doing, Johanna, but as soon as you decide, call me, day or night."

Smitty returned to the station and began looking into Fawad Baqri and noticed that his sister-in-law was just reported missing. Smitty knew in her heart that Fawad had to be involved with this abduction as well, as these types of crimes against women are often committed by those closest to them. She was hoping Johanna would cooperate, to have Fawad charged with his sister-in-law's abduction. The Limitation Act of 1908 provides time limits for crimes committed in Pakistan, so this recent crime could make his imprisonment a sure thing, and Johanna's abduction would be evidence toward his conviction.

CHAPTER 18 – PART OF
THE CONGREGATION

C layton and Azra stood in the kitchen of the farm-house, after Mr. and Mrs. Donovan finished their discussion about Ellen and their work to help her to salvation, and then headed toward the church to greet the congregation before service began. Clayton was visibly shaken by the story the Donovans had just told them, and so was Azra, just not for the same reason as Clayton. Azra was slowly thinking about how she was going to continue to get to know a little girl that would barely speak to her. Azra decided she would begin to slow her work with Clayton, and spend more time working with Ellen on her morning chores as well as her scripture recitations. Azra came with Clayton to Colorado to fulfill one purpose, and now was the time to begin the transition to fulfill her main priority, she just needed a way to bring this up to him.

Clayton, Azra, and Ellen walked together to the barn for the service where everyone would be meeting the new visitors. Clayton was wearing a plain, dark-blue suit, Azra was in her cherry red dress, and Ellen donned the kelly-green dress that was attractive but marred with the memories of her first experience in this renovated church. Since Ellen's rite of sacrifice on the altar, she feared walking into the barn at all, even when there was no one else in the building, but she had no allowance for fear in this situation. Mother and Father saw fear as the most selfish form of weakness in children, and her daily punishments, as well as the service rituals, were all attempts to remove her fear.

Clayton opened the large, heavy door to the converted barn to see the pews almost completely filled to capacity. The group was conversing with Mother and Father, and with one another, until they saw the door creep open and the trio walk through the large entrance. After all, they were the guests of honor and all were anticipating their arrival. Ellen was going to be introducing the two guests. Her presence at the altar would show the congregation that she was fully recovered from her sacrifice, and it would also provide proof that evil can be cured from anyone who seeks redemption.

Mr. Donovan walked to the altar and rang the small bell he carried in church to get the congregation to come to order. Everyone immediately took their seats and provided him with their undivided attention. Mr. Donovan became a very strong force in the community where he had situated his church. Other than the members that had followed the Donovans to Colorado, most were from the small town of Alamosa. The community was already very conservative, and this helped spread the messages of the church to return to the simpler times of devoting every aspect of life to worshipping God, seeking his approval and, eventually, being selected by him to move to the realm of Heaven.

"My dear friends, today we begin the celebration of abundance of the fall harvest as it carries us through the winter season of longer nights and colder days," Mr. Donovan greeted his congregation with a tone of promise and gratitude. He continued, "Miracles are possible when you put your trust in Him, and my daughter, Ellen, is yet another example of that trust." Mr. Donovan motioned toward Ellen to take his place at the altar to introduce Clayton and Azra.

Ellen stood in her father's place, staring out at the congregation as they waited for her to speak. She noticed the dark stain on the wood below Clayton and Azra's feet, the stain that was made from her blood, of which neither of them was aware. Ellen took a deep breath in and proceeded to speak, "This time of year is marked with celebrations all over the world; celebrations that forget the purpose of this season and neglect to honor the gratitude that we owe to God for his bounty." Ellen took an even deeper breath and continued her introduction, "We are grateful for His grace and we plan to share the harvest with our community of worshippers. Please join me in welcoming our guests for the season, Clayton and Sarah."

Clayton and Azra raised their arms in awkward waves and extended eye contact with a large group of people they had never met. Mr. Donovan motioned Clayton and Sarah to their seats in front of where he stood for the remainder of the service. As Mr. Donovan spoke, Clayton remembered his dreams and remembered the sad little girl he was desperately trying to find. He glanced over at Ellen, sitting in her chair with perfect posture, and a blank, empty stare. Clayton knew he needed to talk to Ellen, just to ask her a few questions, to see if she really did need his help or if the recurring dream he had about this place was just one big coincidence, after all.

After the service, the entire congregation waited in line to shake hands with the guests and thank them for their time during the season of abundance. Clayton was exhausted and looked around for his hosts to ask permission to talk to Ellen about her favorite foods. This was only partially the truth, but she was the only person he hadn't spoken to about the feasts he was preparing. Just then, he noticed that Azra and Ellen were making their way out of the barn together. Clayton politely said goodbye to the older gentleman he was speaking to and followed behind the two as they walked from the barn to the house. He watched them enter through the kitchen but, when he opened the back door, they were not in the house. He looked to his left and noticed the basement door was slightly ajar and decided they must have gone into the basement. The light to the basement was not on, and the switch that normally turned the light on wasn't working, so Clayton walked carefully down the stairs in the dark with both hands on either side of the stairwell.

As Clayton reached the bottom of the stairs, he could see a light in a room on the far side of the basement and he could hear voices coming from the room. He slowly walked toward it, trying to keep his presence unknown, to see why the two had run so quickly away from the barn. As he approached the room, Clayton noticed all of the medical equipment setup to serve as a makeshift intensive care unit, or clinic. As he scanned the room in the darkness, he saw the hospital bed and heart monitor from the dream he had during his heart attack. Clayton stopped to examine the bed, mainly the sheets for the bloody message that he received in his dream, but they were clean. Just as he was focused on studying the heart monitor, he heard Azra speaking in a pointed tone, but he couldn't quite make out what she was saying.

As Clayton inched closer and closer to the light, Azra's voice became clearer, "Ellen, have you ever heard of something called the Legacy?" Azra questioned Ellen.

"No, I don't think so, other than knowing some definitions of the word, is...is that what you mean?" Ellen responded, with a slight tone of confusion in her voice.

"How could you not know? Ellen, how can you not know your life's purpose? Why are you lying to me?" Azra questioned Ellen with anger and impatience.

Clayton couldn't see her face, but Ellen's voice was more vulnerable sounding than when she spoke to Mrs. Donovan. He couldn't understand what Azra was doing or what she was talking about.

"I am sorry, Sarah, I wish that I knew how to answer your questions, I am so sorry, Sarah." Ellen began to cry.

"Ellen, you don't know me, and I am *not* who you think I am, but you have to promise to always tell me the truth. Do you understand?" Azra asked Ellen as she stood grasping both of the little girl's shoulders.

"I promise to always tell you the truth!" Ellen replied.

"You must also promise to keep our conversations private. Do you also understand that, Ellen?" Azra again asked Ellen.

"I promise to keep our conversations private, Sarah," Ellen again responded to Azra.

Clayton didn't want Ellen or Azra to notice him, so he quietly moved from the dark basement and back to the barn to turn in for the night. He didn't know what Azra was talking about when she asked Ellen about something called the Legacy. He also never heard her sound so angry. Clayton decided it may be a good idea to meet with Azra first thing in the morning, to make sure she didn't need to talk to him about anything.

The next morning, Azra came to Clayton's room before he had a chance to finish getting ready for the day.

"Clayton, sorry to barge in on you, but I needed to get your permission before I can talk to Mrs. Donovan," Azra spoke with labored breath from running over from the house.

"My permission?" Clayton questioned what Azra just said.

"Yes, I am thinking of making more of a presence in Ellen's life. She doesn't have any friends and I think she could use someone to talk to in the morning while she does her chores," Azra explained. She continued, "If it's ok with you, I was hoping to spend a few mornings a week with her, as long as it didn't interfere with your work."

Clayton didn't have enough time to think about this proposition or about how strange it all seemed after what he witnessed last night in the basement, but this could help him get closer to Ellen, to find out why she was in his dreams. He reluctantly agreed to take on most of the work himself.

"Sure, Azra, that's fine, she seems like a good kid that could use a friend," Clayton remarked.

Azra gave Clayton a hug and ran back toward the house. Clayton wasn't sure what to think about Ellen. He could see that she was lonely, timid, and always ready to please her mother, but he still needed to talk to her, discreetly, and approach her with patience and kindness.

CHAPTER 19 – AZRA'S ACCLIMATION

Azra and Clayton had been at the farm a little over two full weeks. Clayton had been relying less and less on Azra to help him with the food preparation and planning of the feasts, due to her new and unexpected responsibility of mentoring Ellen. Often, Azra would either be egregiously late to their morning meetings to discuss the needs of the day and updates for the week, or she simply made other arrangements during the same time periods to consult with Mrs. Donovan and work with Ellen. Clayton began interacting less with Azra as well; it seemed that she was purposefully distancing herself from him and he wasn't sure why. Azra was attending all three church services a week and she started wearing plain, very modest clothing outside of church. She was also voraciously reading the Puritan bible they both received when they arrived in Colorado several weeks ago. Clayton decided that the next time he saw Azra, he would try to talk to her about what was going on, just in case she needed to talk about anything. He was hoping the exposure to this extreme type of lifestyle wasn't starting to affect her.

Clayton witnessed the harsh reality of the Puritan life and saw evidence of abuse that Ellen may have received at the hands of Mrs. Donovan, in the name of religion. He didn't feel comfortable talking to anyone about the abuse and he really didn't have anyone *to* talk to about it. He never witnessed abuse, first-hand, but it was just something that he could *tell* was going on here at the farm. Clayton couldn't talk to his mother because he hadn't told her about the job at the Donovans, mainly because it could so easily be traced back to his father, and he didn't want to have to lie to her. Clayton knew he would see Azra today, during lunch, since the entire congregation was coming for the long-awaited *Great Winter Feast*. Puritans did not celebrate the Christmas season the same way other religions would mark this time of the year, and the feast was the most important part of the season.

Mr. and Mrs. Donovan believed that modern day Puritans should use this season to extend the gratitude they celebrated during and after the Thanksgiving holiday, through to the Christmas holiday, a full winter of gratitude. The feast provided the congregation a time to see the harvest that would continue to nourish them over the long winter and as a symbol of God choosing them to be worthy enough of such a bountiful feast.

Clayton never discussed religion with the congregation, and no one asked him about his own religious beliefs, either. Mr. Donovan asked Clayton, on his day of arrival at the farm, if he had a relationship with God, and Clayton requested that his personal religious beliefs be kept private for now. Mr. Donovan honored that request, as long as Clayton did not interfere with their practices as practitioners of Puritanism, to which Clayton agreed.

The feast setup began just after lunchtime and Azra came to Clayton to discuss what was needed for her to do before the congregation arrived. She mentioned that she was with Ellen all morning and injured her hand while working with Ellen on her morning chores. Clayton agreed not to ask her to do any heavy lifting but then stopped her right as she was attempting to turn and walk away.

"Azra, I feel like you have been avoiding me lately, are you upset with me about anything?" Clayton nervously forced this question out of his mouth.

"Oh, Clayton, no, there is nothing that I am upset about. I am a little overwhelmed with Ellen and I didn't realize just how much I feel as though I belong here," Azra said without looking once in Clayton's eyes. She continued her seemingly sincere confession, "What I never told you is that I have struggled most of my life and this life seems so simple, and so freeing."

"Do you mean that you are considering *staying* here with the Donovans?" Clayton asked, trying hard not to show his disapproval.

"Well, Mrs. Donovan asked if I would be interested in remaining through to summer as a trial to be Ellen's live in mentor and spiritual guide," Azra replied in a slow, almost apologetic manner.

"But, how can you be a spiritual advisor and not know much about this religion?" Clayton questioned Azra using a harsher tone than he usually did with her.

"Mrs. Donovan explained that mentors in this religion are not selected for their tenure, but for their spirit," Azra answered Clayton's question and continued, "Mrs. Donovan said she can tell that I am special, like Ellen, and that I was preselected by God to be a Puritan."

"Well, I know that you are an adult, and I cannot tell you how to live your life, but I would feel better if you came home with me at the end of January." Clayton decided it was best to just tell Azra how he felt about the unusual proposition she was considering.

"I have time to decide, Clayton. I promise you will be the first to know my decision," Azra said with a comforting smile on her face. "Now let's feed these people, shall we?"

The feast was a great success for the congregation and for the Donovans. The membership to the church was growing quickly and the congregation's tithing had provided more than enough money to continue the growth and allow for the Donovans to hire someone like Azra to help with Ellen.

Initially, Mrs. Donovan didn't know if she would be able to trust Azra with some of the most important forms of punishment that were issued to Ellen, some of the most severe Azra had yet to witness. Mrs. Donovan decided to test her ability to rely on Azra to do the work necessary to keep Ellen progressing into the Puritan that she was meant, and destined, to be (according to Mrs. Donovan's extremely pious viewpoint).

Often, before morning chores, Ellen would be quizzed on the scriptures that she had been struggling with over the previous few days, to ensure that she continued to work on them. Azra and Ellen had just sat down for breakfast, and Mrs. Donovan told Ellen to eat without hesitation as she was being tested before "gracing God's Earth" with her undeserving presence. Ellen knew what this meant; she was never very good at memorizing scriptures, and she began to prepare herself for a morning punishment.

"Yes, Mother, I will be ready to recite my scriptures after breakfast, and I will wait for you in my room," Ellen responded with her usual call-and-response type affirmation.

"Actually, Ellen, we have a new setup for your scriptures this morning. Sarah will be following you up to your room after breakfast for recitation," Mrs. Donovan responded, looking at Azra, raising her eyebrow. "Sarah, would you stay at the table for a minute after breakfast so I can discuss it further with you while Ellen waits for you upstairs?"

Azra understood what she was agreeing to, and so did Ellen; she was agreeing to punish Ellen for her inability to perfectly recite the scriptures from the last few days, chosen at random by Azra. Ellen only successfully recited her scriptures once, and, in turn, was punished almost every morning she had spent in the Donovan house since the church had been completed.

Mrs. Donovan gave Ellen the look that told her to leave the room, and without delay, Ellen made her way upstairs to her bedroom to wait for Azra.

Mrs. Donovan looked at Azra for a short period of awkward silence, then finally broke it. "Sarah, I want you to choose any section you wish for Ellen to remember, as she has had more than enough time to study her entire bible."

Azra knew this was going to be an opportune time for her to try to convince Mrs. Donovan that she would be the perfect person for the job of Ellen's mentor. She needed to get as close to Ellen as possible and that could only happen if Mrs. Donovan was convinced of her ability to carry on with Ellen's *education,* just as she had done.

"If Ellen cannot successfully remember the scriptures that you select, you will have to punish her for her failure," Mrs. Donovan spoke without any emotion.

"Yes, Mrs. Donovan," replied Azra. "What is the punishment that you would like me to use?" she questioned.

Mrs. Donovan coldly responded, "You will place Ellen's hands on the page of the scriptures that she cannot successfully recite, and you will use the switch to whip her hands, one for each line of text she forgets. You will make Ellen count the whips after each strike."

"Ok, Mrs. Donovan, I won't let you, or Ellen, down," Azra obediently replied.

"Let us hope not, Sarah...oh, and you can call me Mother," Mrs. Donovan said as she walked out of the kitchen, not bothering to turn around while she walked away from Azra.

Clayton was walking with extra confidence in his stride, from the washroom, down the second-floor hall of the farmhouse, as the barn's was occupied by a congregation member who stayed the previous night to help prepare for the feast. Clayton was proud of the work he was doing at the farm, and the feast was the largest project he ever completed on his own. As he was making his way to the stairs, he could hear the snap of what sounded like a whip or a switch making contact with a surface, as well as Ellen's soft, weak voice counting after each loud crack. This combination of sounds made Clayton stop completely in his tracks. He began to feel the same chill run up his back that he felt during the dream in which he first discovered Ellen's closet. The sounds got louder and clearer as Clayton turned around and walked toward Ellen's bedroom door.

Snap, "four" ...*Snap*, "five" ...*Snap*, "six" ... *Snap*, "seven," Clayton heard coming from Ellen's room, and just before the next snap, he flung the door open, fearing what he was going to discover.

"Azra! What on Earth are you doing?" Clayton saw Azra standing over Ellen, holding a skinny stick covered in blood, while Ellen knelt before her with her hands face up on an open, ruby-stained bible.

"Get out, Clayton! This is none of your business," Azra screamed at him, breathing as heavily as if she had just exhausted herself in taxing physical exercise.

"No, I will not! Ellen, come here, please," Clayton shouted to Ellen, but she didn't budge or even blink.

"Clayton, Ellen knows this is best for her and Mother has directed me to do it," Azra could barely speak without gasping for air.

"Mother? Who is Mother?" Clayton snapped in disbelief.

"I am," Mrs. Donovan answered from just a few inches behind Clayton.

Clayton quickly turned around and stared at Mrs. Donovan and asked, "Do you condone this abuse, Mrs. Donovan?"

To which she responded, "Clayton, you are witnessing the way in which I choose to discipline my child, which is required of me by my religion."

Clayton stood there, speechless, trying to find the words to follow what she had just said, but couldn't. He didn't fear her, nor did he fear Azra, but everything was happening so quickly that he was at a total loss for words.

Mrs. Donovan took the opportunity to continue

her defense, "I am given license, as a parent, to determine what is reasonable and appropriate for my child."

"Does Mr. Donovan know about this?" Clayton realized the question he was asking after it had already left his lips.

"Of course he does, Clayton, this is how he was raised, and this is how Ellen will raise her children as well," Mrs. Donovan responded as though everyone should know how common it was to beat your child with a switch.

Clayton didn't quite know what to do, so, he looked at Ellen and asked her if she needed help. She simply responded, "No, thank you, sir," without looking at him and without any sign of emotion.

Clayton left the house immediately, went to his bedroom in the barn and closed the door. After lying in bed for a moment, staring up at the ceiling, Clayton burst into tears with the vision of Ellen's small, bloody hands quivering over a bible while she sat motionless in the silence of her own fear and pain. He decided he was going to give the Donovans notice of his resignation tomorrow and leave as soon as he possibly could. Clayton promised he wouldn't question their practices, but today, he realized that he couldn't bear witness to all of them either. Clayton didn't leave his room for the entire day or through the night, and no one came to check on him.

Azra got the job of staying on until the Summer of the upcoming year. Mrs. Donovan was pleased with her obedience and realized that her influence was strong enough to convince others of the ways of their religion. She also planned for Azra to aid in her attempts to ensure the children of the congregation were properly groomed to take the church to a higher level of membership and, possibly, to other communities in Colorado.

Mrs. Donovan could rely on Azra to help the children of the congregation, as long as she remained trustworthy these next few months. What she didn't know, was that Azra had no intention of actually fulfilling the duties of any job description she would make for her; she was only here to kill Ellen and end the Legacy as she believed her purpose dictated, through her understanding of the letter she needed to keep out of the hands of Clayton and Ellen. Azra wasn't *really* interested in the Puritan religion, she was playing along to get closer to the child that she believed held the fate of the human species in her hands.

CHAPTER 20 – THE LETTER

C layton was walking barefoot down the Donovan's long, gravel driveway. Behind him, the farmhouse, the barn and the small shed next to the barn, were all engulfed in flames. The fire was so large, and so hot, that he could feel the heat warming his skin, even though he was a little more than halfway to the Donovan's lane. Clayton turned around to watch the house burn, wondering about Mr. and Mrs. Donovan, Ellen, and Azra, but could see no one running out of the house and could hear no one screaming from within the house. He wasn't sure if anyone was burning, or had already been burned, but he also didn't really seem to care, either way. As soon as Clayton realized what he was doing, he turned around and started running back toward the house. He did care, he didn't want anyone to be burned alive in the fire, especially Ellen. She was only a child, a very sad child, and she deserved to live. She also deserved to be happy and carefree like a child was meant to be at her age.

As Clayton ran toward the flames, he began shouting, "Ellen! Ellen! Wake up, Ellen, get out of the house, Ellen!" but no one came out of the house. Clayton made it to the front door of the farmhouse, kicked it open and ran inside, using his bathrobe to shield himself from the flames as he searched for Ellen. He checked the front room, the kitchen, the basement, the downstairs powder room, and nothing. Clayton took a deep breath and sprinted up the stairs, into the heavy smoke that was rising through the house. He immediately ran to Ellen's room, and saw here there, huddled in the closet, curled up with her arms shielding her head from the smoke. He picked her up, cradled her, and ran down the stairs and out of the house into the damp, cool grass of the front yard. He placed Ellen down and started coughing, feeling his lungs fighting for air that wasn't filled with smoke.

As Clayton coughed and fought to breathe, he looked over at the lifeless child lying in the grass, her eyes completely open with no sign of life left in them. He urgently began trying to revive her with CPR, but she wouldn't respond, no matter how strong his efforts. "Come on, Ellen, breathe, please just breathe," Clayton kept trying and trying with all his strength, but it was no use, she had succumbed to the smoke. He began to cry from disbelief, from exhaustion, from his inability to save her. His cries were suddenly interrupted. He heard something several feet behind where he had found refuge in the grass. He turned around, and there stood Mr. and Mrs. Donovan and Azra, watching him, looking as if they escaped the fire without incident, with a disgustingly smug look on their faces.

"How did you all get out? I checked everywhere,

and no one was in the house but Ellen," he shouted at the three just standing there staring at him.

"What did you do, Clayton?" asked Mrs. Donovan.

"Yes, Clayton, what did you do to our beautiful farm?" Mr. Donovan spoke immediately after Mrs. Donovan.

Now, Azra added, "Clayton, Ellen was just a child and your negligence has killed her and burned everything these poor people have ever worked for."

After Azra's comment, the three began to laugh, harder and harder, pointing at Clayton. Their laughing was loud and manic, as though they were *glad* that Ellen had died in the fire and that their entire farm was destroyed.

Clayton, confused and reeling from everything that just took place, picked up Ellen's limp body and started running down the long driveway, barefoot and unsure of where he was going or how the fire started in the first place. He stopped from exhaustion, carefully placed Ellen on the gravel driveway, and lay down next to her. He closed his eyes, held Ellen's body close to his, and drifted off to sleep.

Clayton opened his eyes, but he was no longer in the driveway. He was back in his bed in the barn that was still standing, just as it was before the fire. He smelled his clothes and they didn't smell at all like smoke. He ran to the door of the barn, peered out and saw that the house was still there, in fact, the morning was calm and quite serene. The sun was about to begin its ascent toward the horizon and Clayton could see the kitchen light was switched on, meaning that Azra, Ellen and Mrs. Donovan were awake and having breakfast. After a few minutes had passed, Azra and Ellen made their way outside, which was not the normal routine for the day. Ellen usually had to recite her scriptures before starting her morning chores. Perhaps yesterday's extreme punishment allowed Ellen a few days to heal both the physical and mental wounds before she was subjected to even more abuse.

Just as Ellen and Azra were walking together to the small shed by the barn, Mr. and Mrs. Donovan were also making their way out of the farmhouse to their sedan parked in the driveway, near the backdoor. As the Donovans pulled away, Azra was helping Ellen set up a large ladder against the house, preparing to wash the exterior glass of each of the windows. Clayton thought about how rare it was that the entire family was out of the house at the exact same time. He also thought about how he was curious to see if Ellen's room was as he saw it in his dreams, but never had the chance to be alone in the house to investigate.

Clayton exited the barn and made his way across the gravel to the back door of the house while Azra held the ladder for Ellen as she began to wash her first set of second floor windows, starting with the Donovans' bedroom. Clayton knew that he wouldn't have much time before Ellen got to her own bedroom window, and he wasn't sure how she would react to seeing him in the room. He thought it would be best to make sure she didn't know he was in the house at all, to prevent it from coming up in conversation with Azra or the Donovans.

He entered the house and immediately ran upstairs to the bedrooms. Clayton got to the top of the stairs to find that Ellen's bedroom door was closed, but Azra's was not. Under normal circumstances, he would never dream of infringing on someone else's privacy, but after what he witnessed yesterday, he needed to understand what was going on in this house and why Azra changed so drastically in such a short amount of time on the farm.

Clayton peered around the corner of Azra's door to be sure that Ellen wasn't yet cleaning her windows and quietly moved inside the plain, mostly empty, room. He wasn't exactly sure what he was looking for but noticed a small bright orange shoe box under the bed that caught his attention almost immediately. Clayton knew that Azra bought a pair of new tennis shoes at the Denver International Airport since she forgot to pack her own before the trip, and he assumed this was the same box. The box lid was slightly ajar, and he could see loose cash and some folded papers inside.

As he was moving toward the box, the ladder that Ellen had been cleaning the windows on slammed against the windowsill outside Azra's bedroom window.

There stood Ellen, on the ladder, looking directly at him. Clayton looked back at Ellen and motioned for her not to say anything by placing his index finger against his lips while Ellen remained motionless, staring at him.

"Are you planning on washing those windows, Ellen, or is there a ghost in my room?" Azra questioned Ellen as she hesitated, after seeing Clayton.

Ellen responded, "Oh, no, sorry, I was just thinking about my scriptures."

Ellen took the freezing cold sponge from the equally freezing cold water in the bucket. It was precariously balancing on one of the steps of the ladder just below Ellen's chin while she proceeded to wash the windows, still glaring at Clayton.

Clayton panicked and just grabbed the entire shoe box and left the room in a hurry. There was nothing else in the room, besides a few articles of clothing, but his curiosity was piqued with the shoebox. He decided that since he knew where Ellen was in her progress with the window washing, he would just take a fast look around Ellen's bedroom closet, but not spend too much time looking for anything else. He really just wanted to compare the reality of the closet to what he remembered from his dreams.

As Clayton slowly opened Ellen's door, an obvious chill hit his skin and he shuddered with a musty smelling frigidness. He quickly walked over to the closet and opened the door. There was nothing in the closet but clothing and shoes, two dresses and two pair of shoes, to be exact. This room, not of his dreams but Ellen's *real* bedroom, actually had a bed in it. It was a small, old cot, but a bed, nonetheless. Also, there were blankets and a pillow on the bed and not in the closet. There weren't drawings in the closet either, as there were in his dreams.

Clayton rushed downstairs and outside to hide the shoebox in his own room, when he was intercepted by the Donovans. They were on their way to the local grocery, to pick up the pre-ordered supplies Clayton requested to prepare the meals for the next few days, when Mr. Donovan realized he forgot his wallet on the kitchen counter.

"Good morning, Clayton, I see that you are feeling better from your episode yesterday morning," Mrs. Donovan said with a raised eyebrow.

"Good morning, Mrs. Donovan, um, well, I would like to talk to you about yesterday, but I need to go back to my room for a second," replied Clayton.

"Nonsense, Clayton, we will talk now. Mr. Donovan and I have been talking about you all morning and we should really try to bury the hatchet as soon as we possibly can before this sort of thing turns into something it shouldn't," Mrs. Donovan responded by gently grasping Clayton's bicep to lead him toward the door from which he just came.

Clayton held the shoebox behind his back and awkwardly walked back into the kitchen, sat down at the dinner table and placed it on his lap, under the table. In his head, Clayton was calculating how long it would take Azra and Ellen to finish washing the windows, put the supplies back into the shed, and make their way back to the house.

Mr. Donovan was about to speak when his wife held up her hand, suggesting he let her speak, and said, "Clayton, we are very concerned with the behavior that you displayed yesterday. It seems that you don't understand the ways of our religion and how we hold children accountable..."

Clayton immediately interrupted her, to speed the conversation along. Besides, he did understand, and he couldn't allow himself to be any part of it. He spoke with urgency, "Mrs. Donovan, with all due respect, I am uncomfortable fulfilling the rest of my obligation here at the farm if I have to pretend to support the abuse of your daughter."

Mrs. Donovan's eyes widened as though someone just slapped her viciously across the face. Mr. Donovan noticed her reaction and decided he needed to interject, "Clayton, do not think that you can sit here, in our house, and accuse us of child abuse when we work tirelessly to raise Ellen as if she was our very own."

"Mr. Donovan, I am sorry for my outburst, I am having a hard time acclimating to the farm and I believe it would be best for me to end my time here early. I mean no disrespect," Clayton responded to try to diffuse the situation as well as hurry it along before Azra and Ellen came back from their work.

"Well, Clayton, if that is how you feel, we can make the arrangements for you to fly back to New York as soon as you would like, but I am afraid that I will have to reduce your salary based on the time you have spent here on the farm," Mr. Donovan explained.

Mrs. Donovan quickly interjected, "...and you will have to pay for the unexpected early departure out of your salary."

"I completely understand, Mrs. Donovan. Again, I meant no disrespect, and I hope you can forgive my outburst," Clayton insincerely requested of Mrs. Donovan.

"Clayton, why don't you take today to think about everything and come back to talk to us before dinner, this evening? Perhaps Mrs. Donovan and I have a few things to discuss as well," Mr. Donovan softened his face and smiled while he spoke.

Clayton was relieved that he was able to now quickly seek refuge in his room before Azra would see that he was holding her orange shoe box. "Thank you, I will, and I appreciate your patience with me." Clayton was lying to the Donovans so he could get out of that kitchen. As he ran across the gravel from the house to the barn, he could see Azra locking up the shed and Ellen dumping her window-washing bucket onto the stones of the driveway.

Clayton rushed into his room and closed the door

behind him. He sat down on the bed and proceeded to take the lid off the brightly colored shoe box that he took from under Azra's bed. Inside the box was what looked like a voice recorder, that doctors sometimes use to dictate notes, a stack of folded cash, and a few white, worn pieces of paper. He took the small recording device and tucked it into his backpack and then counted the $855.00 in cash and placed the wad in his front pocket.

Lastly, he unfolded the papers he found in the box and discovered he was holding a letter. One of the letters was ornately written in a different language, he assumed Chinese, and the other letter was written in English. He placed the letter he couldn't read to the side and began to read the one he could understand.

Clayton sat on his bed, and read the entire letter, but wasn't entirely sure what to think about everything that was contained in it. The name "Ellen" was written in Azra's handwriting and circled at the bottom of the last page. He decided to read it, over and over, thinking about Ellen as he read. The more he thought about Ellen, the more the letter seemed to make sense; she was living a life of pure agony, but why would Azra have this letter in the first place? Was she part of this Legacy the letter was referencing? As he sat and envisioned Ellen within his mind's eye, he could see her standing in front of her window again.

Clayton was seeing her from the front yard, as he often saw her in his dreams, but this time, she was

smiling and waving to him. Clayton wasn't sure exactly
what the letter, or the vision, meant, but he would take
the letter and he would read it to Ellen. Something was
driving him to connect with her since before he arrived.
It was time to stop at nothing to make this happen, especially now with the discovery of this letter. Clayton
also knew he must be cautious of Azra after what he
witnessed yesterday. Does this letter have anything to do
with her insistence to mentor Ellen and stay on after he
was planning on leaving the farm? Clayton was unsure of
who he could trust here on the Donovan farm, and realized that after he spoke to Ellen, he would also try to convince her to go away with him.

CHAPTER 21 – AZRA'S CHOICES

Now that Clayton had the letter in his hands, and a few hours before the Donovans would be expecting him for dinner, he made a plan to wait for Azra to give Ellen some private time to study her scriptures so he could approach her without anyone noticing. Clayton had not had a chance to talk to Ellen alone, and this was a main objective of his since he arrived on the farm.

Clayton broke down the cardboard shoe box and stashed it within his luggage to hide the evidence that he took the box from Azra's bedroom. He carefully maneuvered his way to the back entrance of the house, but as he approached it, he could hear the Donovans and Azra having a conversation on the other side of the door. Clayton changed plans and, instead, quietly entered the house from the front door, to attempt to get to Ellen's room without anyone taking notice. The trio was talking rather loudly about tomorrow's church service while Mr. Donovan practiced part of his sermon for the women. Clayton made it up to Ellen's room, and as she turned around, was startled to see him. He again motioned for her to be quiet as he softly closed her bedroom door behind him.

Clayton explained to the child in front of him what was going on. "Ellen, I am not here to hurt you, I am here to help you." He continued through a wavering, somber voice, "I have a letter here that I believe is meant to be delivered to you.

Clayton unfolded the letter and began to read to her. As he read to Ellen, she gave him all of her attention, as if there was nothing else going on in the entire world. After he finished, Ellen sat and thought about what he just read to her. She looked calm and almost totally confident in what she was supposed to do with the contents of the letter.

"Does this make any sense to you, Ellen?" Clayton asked.

Ellen looked at Clayton and tears started to flow from her tired, sad eyes.

"I think so, Clayton, I think so. I have been waiting so long for you, but I didn't know who you were or what you were going to say to me when you arrived," Ellen said with relief and exhaustion at the same time.

"You have been waiting for *me*?" asked Clayton, remembering the messages that Ellen would leave for him in his dreams.

"I would dream of you coming to the farm, but you would look right through me. You came to me when I was in my closet and you came to me when I was in the hospital bed in the basement, but when I would speak to you, you couldn't see or hear me," Ellen explained to

Clayton.

Clayton began to get emotional, but he was still able to speak through the breaks in his voice. "I have enough money to take us away from here, Ellen. Would you like to come with me?"

She looked at him, as though no one had ever shown her any kind of compassion before this very moment, "Where will we go?"

"I will take you to the police, Ellen, but you will have to tell them about the abuse," Clayton responded with a look of great affection in his eyes, which brought Ellen the comfort she needed during a time like this.

Just as Clayton was gathering some of Ellen's things, Azra pushed open her bedroom door to find out why she hadn't been downstairs to begin her afternoon chores.

"Ellen, I have been downstairs waiting for you... oh, Clayton, what on Earth are you doing in here?" she was completely taken off-guard with Clayton's presence in Ellen's bedroom. "Why are you packing some of Ellen's things?" she asked as she observed him.

"Azra, I am taking Ellen with me, she isn't safe here and she wants to leave," Clayton indignantly answered Azra.

"What? Ellen, where did you get those papers you are holding?" Azra noticed Ellen holding the letter that she thought was safely hidden in her bedroom. "Did you get that from the shoe box in my room?"

"Um...no, no, I...," Ellen struggled to answer Azra's question, without incriminating Clayton in the process.

Clayton noticed Ellen's attempt to protect his secret, "I took it, and I gave her the letter. We know everything, Azra," The size of the lump in his throat was growing by the second.

"What? Why were you in my room?" Azra looked at Clayton with narrowed eyes, waiting for a response that would make sense of everything.

Clayton took one of the deepest breaths of his life and said, "Azra, after yesterday's incident, I wanted to find out what was going on with you. You just aren't the same person that I met before coming here."

As Azra's face began to twist and change, she walked over to Ellen and tore the letter out of her hands and told her to wait in her closet.

"No, Ellen, you don't have to do that any longer, you aren't a prisoner here anymore," Clayton spoke in a demanding tone and with a volume that was heard by the Donovans downstairs.

"Sarah...Clayton...what is going on up there?" Mr. Donovan yelled as he walked from the kitchen to the stairs.

Clayton moved toward Ellen to keep her safe from Azra as she motioned toward her. Mr. Donovan's footsteps were getting louder as he made his way from the first floor while the uncomfortable situation unfolded upstairs.

"Get away from her, Clayton, you have no idea what you are doing," Azra spit out her demand with a look of pure evil on her pale face.

"Azra, you have changed, and you need to just let us get away from here. No one will think you had anything to do with Ellen leaving the farm. You have to stop this," Clayton pleaded with Azra in a mournful tone.

"I will never let her get away, I need to do what I came here to do," she responded.

Just as Azra completed her confession to Clayton, she pushed him away from her and took Ellen by the hair and rushed her out of the bedroom toward the stairs.

Azra didn't have a moment to think about what she was doing, and she believed that no matter what happened to her, she had to fulfill her destiny as the Imbalance chosen to end the human race. Mr. Donovan was standing, halfway to the second floor, while he watched Azra's gaze fixed on the stairs, and then on Ellen, and then, back to the stairs. He shouted toward Azra as she made the split-second decision to throw the child over the threshold, before either of the men were able to intervene.

Ellen's thin body was lifted off of the ground with the painful tug of a handful of golden hair in Azra's hands. Ellen initially came crashing down on the second wooden step from the top, but then continued her way down, rolling violently from step to step, each step accompanied by the thud of her small head.

"No! Sarah!" Mr. Donovan shouted as Ellen's body came crashing at his feet, knocking him backward and down the rest of the stairs. His body crashed down much harder than Ellen's, ending at the front door of the house, with an unmistakable crack of his neck. Clayton ran toward Azra and delivered her a left hook directly to the face, rendering her unconscious as she fell to the floor.

Clayton rushed to where Ellen's body stopped on the stairs and gently picked her up, cradled her body, and raced toward the kitchen. Mrs. Donovan stood in the kitchen, holding a butcher knife, when Clayton entered with her daughter's limp body.

"Put her down, Clayton, she belongs with her mother," Mrs. Donovan was obviously nervous and unsure of how to deal with him.

"She's dead, Mrs. Donovan, and you're partly to blame," Clayton shouted at her while he cried over Ellen's body in his arms.

Mrs. Donovan allowed Clayton to move past her, and she stood there, watching him struggle to open the door and run out into the gravel toward the barn. She looked down the hall from the kitchen, seeing her dead husband by the front door, and looked at the knife in her hands, realizing that Clayton would go to the police and she would be held responsible for the abuse of her now dead daughter. Mrs. Donovan may have been a strict disciplinarian and under the belief that children must be punished severely to stay on the right path for salvation, but she was not a cold-blooded murderer.

Mrs. Donovan took the knife she was holding in her hand while standing over the kitchen sink and dragged the blade of the knife along her neck, from the left earlobe to the right. A crimson fountain of blood filled the sink and spilled down the front of her housedress. Her body fell to the ground, lifeless and alone.

Clayton ran, with Ellen still in his arms, into the barn to grab the money he took from Azra. He closed and locked his bedroom door, in case Azra was to regain consciousness before he was safely out of the barn and off the property. As he was gathering the essentials, and Azra's cash, Ellen began to wheeze and cry, "Clayton, what happened?" she was able to softly speak to him.

"Ellen! You're alive! Are you in pain?" Clayton questioned in disbelief.

"Yes, I think there is something wrong with my ribs," she responded while struggling to breathe.

"Ellen, I am so sorry for everything you've gone through, and I promise nothing like this will ever happen to you again." All of Clayton's sorrow and sadness were pouring out with his words as he pleaded with Ellen to feel safe with him. "People are good, and kind, and decent. You have to know that you deserve to be loved and you deserve to be safe," he said as he held her and cried harder than he had ever cried before in his life.

Ellen felt the strength of Clayton's arms wrapped around her. For the very first time in her life, felt safe and

loved. Even though she was in terrible pain from her injuries, his words made her feel that she could trust him
and that he wouldn't allow her to be harmed by anyone, ever again. Ellen didn't want Clayton to cry and feel
the sorrow that he was feeling, so she mustered up the
strength to try to make him feel better, "Clayton, thank
you for helping me and I know you won't let anything
else happen to me."

The truth was, Ellen did feel that way. She wasn't
afraid while in his arms. She was comforted by him, by
the first person in her short life, and she trusted him.
Ellen felt a weight lift from her tiny, burdened shoulders
as she gazed into Clayton's caring and watery eyes.

As the two embraced and cried, as if they were the
only people left on the planet, Clayton began to smell
smoke.

"Ellen, do you smell that?" he asked, "Does it smell
like smoke to you?"

Ellen, noticing the caustic smoke billowing in
from under the door, immediately alerted Clayton,
"Clayton, the door, look!"

Clayton picked up Ellen and told her to hide her
face against his chest while he kicked the bedroom door
open and rushed out into the church area of the barn,
where he saw Azra, standing by the large door of the barn
with a gas can, from the shed, in her hands.

"Looks like you're at a dead end, Clayton," Azra
said with a smile on her face.

Clayton, unable to breathe with the smoke filling the entire room, shouted back to her, "It's too late, Azra. Ellen fulfilled the purpose of the Legacy, it's time to give up," he said as he choked and coughed.

"I don't feel any different, Clayton, as an Imbalance I would know if the Legacy had been fulfilled." Azra smirked as she swung the gas can like a gleeful child. Just then, Azra threw the gas can toward the flames on the altar and escaped from barn through the large door.

Clayton turned and noticed that the gas landed directly into the hottest, bluest flames. He turned back around, now facing the door, and ran as fast as he could while struggling to keep his footing, with Ellen holding on as tightly as possible.

Clayton opened the door, and standing just inches from him, was Azra, holding a shot gun that she stole from the house.

"Give her to me, Clayton," Azra demanded.

"Never, you will have to kill me before you kill her," he said without fear.

Just as Azra raised the shotgun to shoot Clayton, the barn was engulfed by a ball of fire from an explosion within the church, throwing all three of their bodies several feet into the gravel, knocking them unconscious.

CHAPTER 22 – NEW BEGINNINGS

C layton opened his eyes and noticed that he must have been knocked unconscious from the blast. He managed to get back onto his feet, but his leg was badly burned, and he was in a great deal of pain. As he limped around where the barn stood just moments before the explosion, he could hear Ellen calling after him.

"Ellen, where are you, Ellen!" he called in response to her cries. Her voice was coming from the house, which had caught fire from the burning debris of the barn explosion. Clayton used every ounce of strength he could find within himself to run toward the back door of the house and find her. Ellen had run inside, thinking that both Clayton and Azra had perished from the explosion, and went to the only place where she ever felt safe, her bedroom closet. That is where Clayton found her, alert and awake enough to grasp her arms around his neck as he carried her down the stairs to safety.

Clayton placed Ellen gently on the cold grass, and then remembered Azra was lying in the driveway and she could still be in danger from both structures burning around her. He couldn't just let her potentially burn to death, even if she was the one that caused all of this pain and suffering; he couldn't, in good conscience, let her die that way.

Clayton ran around to the back of the house to find Azra awake and rubbing her dirty face with her even dirtier hands. She looked at him calmly, her face softer than it had ever been, and she didn't struggle when he reached for her. Clayton was confused by the sudden change in her demeanor. Azra didn't say anything to Clayton, in fact, she looked as though she really didn't know what was going on, at all.

The three sat in the grass, and watched the house burn to the ground, as sirens screamed up the gravel driveway. The house was burning with a brilliance that the three of them had never seen before in their lives. They didn't speak to one another, but they didn't feel as though they needed to say anything at all. Ellen looked at Azra, "Sarah, is that you?" she asked.

"It is, Ellen, it is," Sarah spoke in her true voice for the very first time since arriving at the Donovan farm.

Clayton looked past Ellen and toward Sarah, and said, "What happened to Azra?"

"I don't know," Sarah said in a confused, but relieved, tone, "I think she's gone."

The three looked at one another, smiling, as they were surrounded by fire trucks, ambulances and police cars, with men and women in uniform rushing from their vehicles to get to them as quickly as possible.

Johanna was released from the psychiatric institution and living in a group home with three other women recently released from prison, looking for a fresh start from their former lives of pain and difficult choices. Detective Smitty told Johanna she would arrange to help her go back to Pakistan to be reunited with her family, but she realized that her new life was a gift, and it would be too painful to go back to the neighborhood where she once had a husband and a son that were no longer part of her life.

All of the women sharing the home served their time with no infractions and were all released early due to their rehabilitation while serving their sentences. Johanna was happy in her new home and finally felt as though her life would begin to get better. No longer did Johanna have to worry about her past or the husband that sold her into a life of sex work, but now she could pursue her own interests and dreams. She shared her delayed start in life with the other women in the house, and together, they all worked to find one another jobs and pursue interests that kept them clean, sober, happy and healthy.

Johanna was set up to interview with a clinic nearby, treating patients with dementia and other neurological disorders, as a certified nursing assistant that would pay for her to receive the training and license necessary to, one day, continue on to her registered nursing license. The interview went very well, and she was even offered the position as the meeting came to an end.

"Thank you for coming in today, Johanna, we would like to extend an offer of employment to you and would like you to begin working on Monday morning," said the nursing supervisor to Johanna as she was getting ready to leave.

"Thank you, I appreciate this opportunity and I will be here on Monday," replied Johanna. Johanna picked up her jacket and shoulder bag, turned to her new supervisor and said with a raised eyebrow and a smirk of confidence, "but, please, call me Azra."

Made in the USA
Columbia, SC
31 July 2020